HIS SECRET BABY

A BAD BOY BILLIONAIRE ROMANCE.

MICHELLE LOVE

HOT AND STEAMY ROMANCE

CONTENTS

Sign Up to Receive Free Books	v
1. Chapter One	1
2. Chapter Two	6
3. Chapter Three	11
4. Chapter Four	15
5. Chapter Five	22
6. Chapter Six	27
7. Chapter Seven	34
8. Chapter Eight	38
9. Chapter Nine	47
10. Chapter Ten	51
11. Chapter Eleven	57
12. Chapter Twelve	59
13. Chapter Thirteen	65
14. Chapter Fourteen	71
15. Chapter Fifteen	80
Sign Up to Receive a Free Book	83
Preview of Saving Her Rescuer	84
Chapter one	87
Chapter Two	93
Chapter Three	101
About the Author	111

Made in "The United States" by:

Michelle Love

© Copyright 2020 – Michelle Love

ISBN: ISBN: 978-1-64808-077-7

ALL RIGHTS RESERVED. No part of this publication may be reproduced or transmitted in any form whatsoever, electronic, or mechanical, including photocopying, recording, or by any informational storage or retrieval system without express written, dated and signed permission from the author

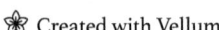 Created with Vellum

SIGN UP TO RECEIVE FREE BOOKS

Sign Up to Receive Free E-Books and Audiobook Codes.

Would you like to read **The Unexpected Nanny, Dirty Little Virgin** and **other romance books** for **free**?

You can sign up to receive these free e-books and audiobooks by typing this link into your browser:

https://www.steamyromance.info/free-books-and-audiobooks-hot-and-steamy/

Or this one:

https://www.steamyromance.info/the-unexpected-nanny-free/

BLURB

Five years ago, my father died when his car's brakes gave out on a cliffside road just outside Monterey. It was no accident. Armand Rossini, high-ticket international assassin, replaced my father's mechanic that day and did something to that car. And I've been hunting him ever since.

But now that I've caught him ... why can't I tear my eyes away from him? How can I be so attracted to the man who killed my dad? And why is he trying to tell me that I'm in danger?

One hot night of passion and some really ugly truths turn my world upside down as I realize that neither Armand nor my father were the people I thought. But when I find out I'm carrying the assassin's child, it's not the only revelation that rocks my world. It turns out that Dad wasn't the only one in the family who was keeping secrets.

1
CHAPTER ONE

Marina

The nightmares come just when they always do. It's five in the morning and I find myself once again sitting up shaking as chills of terror rack my body. I press my fist against my lips reflexively, stifling a scream so that it comes out only as a tiny squeak. For a few moments, I ball up, face between knees, shivering. But then the sweet-spicy smell of scented candles brings me back to reality.

I look around as I catch my breath. I'm in my room, in my home, safe. The vast chamber is empty except for me. The polished brass of my bedframe gleams in the moonlight spilling through my bedroom windows.

Everything is still; peaceful. But I'm bathed in cold sweat and my chest hurts from how hard my heart is beating. And yet I can't remember anything about the dream that put me into such a state.

Crap. Again. I wrap the wool comforter closer around me and huddle under it, breathing deeply until the shaking stops. This happens at least a few times a week, but I've never managed to get used to it, even after five years. These dreams have been haunting me since James Shea, my father, died.

Seething with frustration over my interrupted sleep and the terror I can't do anything about, I get up and change into a sports bra and yoga pants. *At least this time I managed not to scream aloud and wake up Uncle Bradley.*

Uncle Bradley is another fixture of the last five years. He moved in right after Father's murder, and I've been living with him ever since. I don't technically need a guardian anymore, but after five years, I've gotten pretty used to having him around. It was a real comfort at first—and a necessity, as I was only fifteen then, when he volunteered to be my legal guardian.

It's a little awkward now that I'm a grown woman, but he insists on keeping an eye on me. If I scream too loud, his tall, chubby form will come shoving through my doorway, never knocking, his robe flapping around him and his small gray eyes focused on me like lasers.

It's a good thing I've never felt inclined to start sleeping in anything sexy, or to bring a boyfriend home. That would definitely make everything even more awkward, especially considering Uncle Bradley's nosiness. He always wants to know everything that I'm doing, but I forgive him because I know damn well why he's so overprotective.

He's the one who had to come home and break the news to me after that assassin sabotaged my dad's car. He's the one who helped me get through it all, even when the trauma left my memories in tatters. We're the only members of the family left, now that Mom's left the country, and I know he worries about losing me too.

I'm really not sure what I would have done without him, so I don't mind a little intrusiveness. But not when I'm trying to sleep.

I unroll my exercise mat over the muted pink-and-green

carpet, and start my stretches. Sometimes yoga can help me relax enough to fall back to sleep. If that doesn't work, I'll go straight to combat practice so I don't waste any time.

I've always been pretty athletic, but I didn't start intensive training until after Dad died. I knew basic self-defense and had practiced yoga since I was twelve, but I didn't start learning Kali until the moment I stood at his graveside, back when I made my most important promise.

"Uncle Bradley's shown me the evidence, Father. I know your death wasn't an accident. I'll find the man that sabotaged your car, and I'll bring him down. I swear, Daddy, I'm going to send him wherever you are so you can personally kick his pretty Italian ass every day of the afterlife."

It's harder to get in a good session without my practice dummy, but I know better than to drag it out of my closet right now. The grunts and thuds will bring Bradley out of a sound sleep.

He's a strange guy, Uncle Bradley. He's kind but smothering, protective but disinterested in the details of my life. He's also supportive of my efforts to avenge his brother, but is weirdly unwilling to understand my need to get fighting fit before I face my father's murderer.

Striking out at open air, shadow-boxing in the scant moonlight shining on my wall through the windows, I think hard about Armand Rossini. About how I'm going to destroy him.

Armand Rossini is a man who's been on my mind almost constantly for the last five years. The unusually handsome garage attendant first caught my eye when Dad brought his blue Mercedes in for maintenance, but he has my attention now for a much different reason. He was the one who worked on Dad's car. It was that same car that Dad was driving up the mountain alone, fresh from the garage, when the brakes suddenly gave.

We sued the garage and demanded all the information they

had on their "new employee," who had suddenly disappeared after the accident. Everything the garage had turned out to be false.

He was the one. Uncle Bradley confirmed it. Rossini wasn't a mechanic at all, but one of Interpol's most wanted—a killer for hire who specializing in sabotage.

I remember that moment when I first saw Rossini. I was fifteen and full of hormones, and when I glimpsed his dark curls shining in the sun and the white flash of his grin as he talked to a coworker, I thought he was the most beautiful man I had ever seen. For a moment, he turned his dancing black eyes to me ... and I felt like I was falling into their warm depths.

The crush was instant, and so powerful that I had my first erotic dream that night. I woke flustered and warm, but smiling. I daydreamed about him until the night I found out what he had done.

I've hated myself for a long time for that stupid crush. I still feel like a fool for it—especially because I've never been able to get those sexy dreams to go away. Over the years, I've learned to distract myself by planning my father's revenge.

I knew early on that it had to be me. Between his heart condition and his growing alcoholism, Uncle Bradley can't handle the problem directly. And no one else will help us outside Bradley's web of bribed contacts.

The police won't believe us. The FBI and Interpol will do nothing with the lead, even though they've both been chasing Rossini for almost two decades, because they have never able to prove exactly what happened. When I made that oath over my father's grave, it was because there was no one else left to seek justice for his death.

I tested out of high school and started training. I learned to hack, cracking passwords and mining for information online. I learned Italian, Spanish, and Portuguese, as they were all languages that Rossini was fluent in, along with English. Every scrap of information about him that Uncle Bradley passed on to me, I found a way to use in my training.

Now, as I work my way through a series of strikes with my practice knife, the only thing breaking the silence are my soft gasps for air. I won't wake him. He has no idea how long and hard I practice, or how good I've gotten.

Nobody does. The most powerful thing about a secret weapon is that it's a secret.

I felt like a ridiculous klutz for the first six months of practicing. By a year in, I developed a competent grasp of the basics, but I didn't start feeling confident about my combat skills until three months ago though, when I finally managed to disarm my instructor.

Oberst called it a lucky shot, but I saw the frustration in his face as he picked up his practice sword. I'm glad. He was the one who told me I wouldn't take this seriously enough. I swore he'd eat his words. Now he has.

Now I need to make sure that I strip Armand Rossini of more than just his weapon.

I guess I shouldn't have expected I'd be able to sleep a full night. After all, today is the day that my uncle finally found Armand. According to our information, he's been holed up in an ancient, partly-refurbished plantation house in Georgia.

My packed bags wait beside my bed. Our pilot will be flying me out to Atlanta in the morning, where I'll grab a rental car. I'll reach his area before sunset and start scouting.

The prospect of taking a human life makes me sick to my stomach, especially if I get caught. I don't want to go to jail, and I don't want to stain my hands with human blood either.

But not even our vast amounts of money have been able to buy justice from law enforcement. So now I'm going to Georgia, to hunt it for myself.

CHAPTER TWO

Armand

"She left the airport at eight this morning. She'll be in your area by early afternoon."

The man on the phone is using a cheap voice disguiser that does nothing to hide his identity from a trained ear. But I play along with his game of anonymity, even as disgust at his cowardice turns my stomach. I *was* having a lovely morning—until this pig called me up with his kill order.

"What the hell did you do, *stronzo*?" I snap. "I told you that we're done, now that you've broken our agreement. I'm not killing that innocent girl for you."

A low chuckle punctuates the silence on the other end of the line. "Oh, I think you will, considering she's a material witness against you and now knows where you live. You won't have a choice when she shows up on your doorstep."

It's been this way for five years. Ever since I put an end to that beast James Shea, the man who hired me keeps pestering me about "the rest of the work" that he'd ordered. I agreed to both hits initially, hoping he was hiring me to take out both Shea and his unnamed partner.

But then I discovered that the second target was someone else—and killing that someone would go against the guidelines that I gave that fucker the moment I agreed to the job.

"There's always a choice," I reply flatly, and listen to the way his high titter of amusement is distorted by the low-toned disguiser.

A man like me has to have a personal code, or he'll go crazy really fast. My code says no innocents and no kids. Marina Shea, daughter of James, and the only person involved in the hit who saw my face, would already be dead if it wasn't for my code. She *was* a witness, after all.

But the man on the phone wants her dead for his own reasons. It makes me absolutely sick. This waste of skin should know better than to test me on an ironclad promise. I refused to complete the job, even wired him two thirds of his money back—it's not like I need it. But this guy just won't let it go.

"Oh, come now, Armand. You're wanted in ten countries. Your ridiculous code won't keep you alive if the girl or I decide to take you down, and you know it. So just say "yes, sir," finish your kill list, and then you'll never hear from me again."

I was trying to be kind before now, for the sake of the girl. I should have just tracked him down and put a bullet in him for trying to con me into spilling innocent blood. James Shea was in no way innocent. But his daughter?

I still remember her at fifteen—cute and a little gawky, too young for beauty. Coffee-colored hair, big, innocent green eyes. She stared at me, whenever she thought I wasn't looking, with a wide-eyed, dazzled smile that was charming and awkward at once.

Yes, you're cute. You're far too young for me. Bye, now.

She looked at me like I hung the moon. Me, who was about to arrange for her father's untimely but completely deserved death. The irony makes my stomach clench whenever I think about it. I've never felt so guilty about killing a monster before.

I looked at her then, so young and sweet, and thought to myself what a shame it was that she had no idea what her father was. One of the reasons I choose my assignments so carefully, now that I'm wealthy enough to have that luxury, is because I know that when I kill, I don't just end one person. I hurt those close to them too.

We all do. Assassins, soldiers, executioners, any cop who pulls the trigger instead of bringing someone in alive. We don't just kill one individual. We wound families. So I am very careful who I target.

"I understand that you are sending the girl to an address that you believe is connected to me. But I also know that I have five current addresses in the United States alone, and that it will take a tremendous stroke of luck for your investigators to determine which one I'm occupying."

I pause to let this sink in and pour myself a touch more champagne. I drop a frozen strawberry into it—Georgia heat has me parched.

The bastard found the right hideout completely by chance, and now he's sending his second target to my doorstep with a gun and a vendetta. Furious little Marina doesn't know what her father did, or why I agreed to kill him. And so she hates me, and wants me dead.

I wish I could tell her the truth about everything, but she'd never believe me. I look out over the rolling lawn toward the palmettos that border my backyard. *What the hell should I do?*

"You're bluffing," he grumbles, but I hear the shake in his voice and know I have put some doubt in him.

Good. If I'm lucky, he'll call the girl home. If I'm not, I'll have a problem on my hands that I'll have to deal with one way or another.

"Between the two of us, I am the more experienced and skilled in these matters. You may be wealthy and have some clever people on your payroll, but that simply isn't enough. The girl will find nothing but an empty house."

I hear his hard breathing and realize that I've pissed him off. Good. If he's angry, he's even more likely to make a stupid mistake.

But then I hear a beep from the laptop that lies open on the desk in front of me. It's from a blind email address and contains a single file. I check it, then open it—and freeze, staring at my screen.

The man on the phone just sent me a photo of Marina Shea, taken a week ago. Now I've got two reasons to refuse to kill her. *Oh, God.*

The cute little teen who I felt sorry for on that fateful day so many years ago has grown up, filled out, and gotten *stacked*. Her frizzy brown hair now falls in sleek waves, her green eyes are lined with black, and full lips are painted a dark blood red. The black sweater, jeans, and leather jacket are supposed to make her look tough, but the denim clings to her sculpted, powerful thighs and lush hips in a way I can't ignore.

My cock is suddenly so hard that I can't think straight. The voice on the phone is barking threats while I'm staring at the photo of woman he wants dead and wondering if there's any chance at all that I can convince her to stop hating me.

"I could just tell her the truth."

Another long silence. "What truth?" he splutters.

"You've been checking up on me," I say quietly, without revealing a bit of what I have actually learned. "I have also been checking up on you. You know as well as I do that the girl is aware that someone hired me. What would happen if she found out that it was you?"

"She'll never believe you," he stammers quickly. "Never! I

have her twined around my finger and I have for years. You'll have to kill her. You'll have to kill her to save yourself!"

We'll see, I think as he hangs up in my ear. He's just made the mistake of pissing off Armand Rossini for the final time.

The girl's life is in no danger at all, unless I have no other choice. But the man who sent her? His days are numbered.

CHAPTER THREE

Marina

"Yeah, Uncle Bradley, I made it to Atlanta just fine, and I checked in at the hotel." I flop back onto the gold satin bedspread of the too-posh room Bradley arranged, and heave an enormous sigh. "I'll be scouting the address tonight."

"Careful, sweetheart, don't go in too tired. Davies already told me what rough weather you had on the flight from Denver." His voice is warm and kind, but with a warning in it.

"I'll get a meal and a nap in first." And a shower.

The three-hour flight from Denver didn't bother me much, even with all its turbulence. Atlanta traffic in a suddenly balmy sixty-five degrees, while still half dressed for Colorado winter, was forty-five minutes of stifling stop-and-go hell. My body, used to shivering its way through every walk outside, is now dehydrated and sticky.

"Very well. Let me know when you get back. I'll be waiting on your call, dear." He hangs up the phone, leaving me sitting there a moment with a smile frozen on my face.

My stomach jumps around as I strip down for my shower. Tonight, if I'm very lucky, I'll finally get my showdown with Rossini.

There's absolutely no way he'll expect me to have tracked him down. After all, I'm nothing but his victim's grieving kid. He probably hasn't spared a single second of thought on me since the moment he murdered my father. He definitely won't know what I look like anymore.

But I know him. Every line of his beautiful body, of his handsome, hateful face, is burned into my head. That afternoon that he waited for us at the garage, he laughed with his temporary new friends, full of false good cheer. Thinking of it now, I damn myself for the blush of first attraction I felt back then, and try to imagine putting a bullet between those bottomless dark eyes.

The worst part of it all is that I have never been able to shake my attraction to Dad's murderer. I don't know what sick, messed up part of me is responsible for this flaw, but it's true. As I lather up and scrub off in the shower, hands roaming over my body, I think of his effect on me with a mix of desire and self-disgust.

What kind of girl discovers that her type is the man who killed her father? What kind of woman finds herself comparing any man who shows interest in her to that single glimpse of a murderer, laughing falsely with sunlight glinting in his hair? Me, apparently—and I feel like a freak for it.

This guy wrecked my life ... or at least what I can remember of it. My therapist says that I have dissociative amnesia. Basically, I have a lot of memories that are just ... missing.

The blank spots mostly involve my life with my dad. I can remember what I wore on my thirteenth birthday, or how abandoned I felt when Mom walked out on us. I can remember being in the car with my dad when I saw Armand—but I can't remember what we did before that, or after.

I can't remember my father's smile. I can't remember the fun things we must have done together back when I was a kid, or what happened between him and Mom that made her leave. I can barely remember the sound of his voice. But I know he must have been a good man, and that I must have loved him very much, for his loss to have done this to my mind.

My therapist, Dr. Weiss, has been using hypnotherapy to try and to help me piece together what I'm missing, but it doesn't really help. I come out of his sessions feeling calmer, but not remembering a thing more than when I got in. All he is really good for is reassurance.

But even he can't help me get over this fucked up attraction to Armand. I'm so ashamed of it that I've never been able to bring it up.

I start washing my hair, the itch in my scalp dying as soon as the warm water rinses the sweat away. *Next time I change climates, I'm changing clothes on the plane*, I grumble silently to myself.

My hands roam down to scrub the rest of my body and I can't help but think of Rossini once more. The man not only ruined my memories of my father, but he single-handedly ruined my sex life as well. As I grew up and got curves and boys and men started noticing me, I never felt any attraction to any of them. Part of it was that teenage boys are idiots, and men who want teenage girls are predators. I didn't want to have anyone like that in my life.

But some boys might have deserved a chance ... if I could have felt even the tiniest spark of attraction to them. Instead, I felt absolutely nothing, not even for the cute ones. My body wouldn't respond to them, and my mind found them all ... boring.

I won't lie and say that this desire for Armand isn't part of the reason I want him dead. If I kill him, his corpse will be my last memory of him. There's nothing sexy about a corpse.

I would rather remember him as grotesque or chilling than

keep having these thoughts ... and feelings ... and dreams. The dreams are the worst. As I dry off my hair, exhaustion from my short but grueling trip making my eyes ache. I hope that my nap is dreamless.

CHAPTER FOUR

Marina

I hope in vain. When the dreams do come, though, they're not about Armand.

"You need to stop being afraid of the basement, Marina, honey." Dad's voice sounds more annoyed than kind. *The road we're on weaves up the cliffside road to our estate on the mountaintop. The view of the drop-off normally makes me dizzy, but this time I don't care.*

I'm busy thinking about the incredibly cute mechanic that Dad and I left the Mercedes with. Off in the distance, the lights of Denver are flickering on in the growing dusk. But his mention of the basement sends a cold thread of fear through me.

"Sweetie, this is ridiculous. You just had some nightmares, like your therapist said. Just that and some sleepwalking. There's nothing down in the basement to be afraid of." Once again, the words are kind, but his tone has a hard, strident note, as if he's disgusted with me.

"I'm afraid of spiders too, but I don't hear you yelling at me about that," I grumble sullenly, trying to ignore how fast my heart is beating. The black rectangle of the cellar door yawns in my mind, and I

think of the mechanic's dazzling smile instead, trying to push out any other thoughts.

"Spiders bite. Cellars store your wine. One fear's sensible, the other's ridiculous." *The annoyance in his voice lashes me like a whip; I flinch.*

"It's only been a month," I mumble.

He sighs in exasperation. "We all feel bad about your mom leaving, honey, but you need to get over it. Crying in front of guests when I send you down to get a bottle for the table is not acceptable."

"I'm sorry," I almost whisper, resenting him with my whole heart.

"Never mind, young lady. I had just better see some progress soon." *He's pulling onto the stretch of road where the police found the break in the safety barrier, and in the weird way that only dreams work, dream, reality, and memory all seem to combine for a moment.*

I tense, something in me remembering the pitiful mass of crushed metal far below that the Mercedes dream-me is in will become.

"You can't go forever without putting together the pieces. This doesn't begin or end with the Italian. He's just an errand boy, honey" *He's gone off-script suddenly. It's his same voice, the same disgusted tone I remember him using whenever he was disappointed in me. But I somehow know that he's never said these words before.*

"Who hired Armand Rossini? That's my real killer."

I sit up in sudden shock, my wide eyes staring blankly into the room that is now lit only by the glow of the city through the windows. A glance at the clock confirms that I was out for hours. That alone doesn't make any sense; I don't sleep deeply any more. Back home, in my own bed, I get maybe five broken hours, interspersed between the nightmares and dirty dreams, and wake at the slightest sound.

I check my watch. Four solid hours of sleep when I expected to get only one. It's like a damn miracle, but it also leaves me more disoriented than I need to be for my plans.

Am I in any shape to do recon tonight? I almost feel like I must be getting sick. I never sleep that deeply. *And what was it with that dream?*

It wasn't dirty, and it wasn't a nightmare. Unlike some of the crazy dreams of the last five years, there is one element of it that I have trouble accepting as real.

As I sit there, rubbing my temples, I think on that element, and am not sure how to take it. Bradley told me I adored Dad. My therapist said that I act like someone who lost someone dear to her.

But the man in the dream seemed annoyed by not only my fear, but my grief over Mom's leaving. He seemed poised to mock every little sign of weakness—even my inexplicable fear of the basement. He made me feel not only small, weak, and whiny, but also as if my very existence was an inconvenience to him.

The resentment I felt in the dream felt absolutely real. Most teen girls resent their parents at least some, but this was bitter and dark, and full of years of unexpressed fury.

No wonder Mom left if you were such a dick. I just wish I knew why she left me with you.

Except for the yawning cellar door and that heart-freezing terror, I remember absolutely nothing about the night my mother left. I have her phone number and her forwarding address in Mallorca, but every time I try to call her, my stomach knots up and I have to stop before it rings more than twice.

I need to eat, get my focus back, and get that recon of Rossini's property done. He might not even be there, but either way, I need to know the lay of the place if I'm going to have any chance of infiltrating it.

Maybe it would be better if he isn't there tonight. I'm not a coward, and I'd love to just get this whole mess over with. But I need every edge I can get against this guy, and I know it.

I force myself to eat a lean meal of salmon, vegetables, and brown rice. I drink lots of water, making sure I'm hydrated. It's the same kind of food I've been on for years. It helps keep my head clear when I'm expecting to get some exercise—which I am tonight, even if all I end up doing is climbing a fence and sneaking around Rossini's property.

At eleven sharp, my uncle's courier arrives at the hotel with my gear, a nondescript man in a gray suit. I eye the two duffel bags for a few minutes before unzipping them and going through the contents.

As I stare down at them, a wave of apprehension hits me. I'm an idiot. I have five years of combat training and I'm going up against a man who has been killing people for longer than I have been alive. Who am I trying to fool?

It will take more luck than I have ever experienced in my life for me to kill Armand Rossini. It will take even more luck for me to do so without losing my own life in the process. But instead of doing the smart thing and hiring a professional to do the job, I have been obsessed for years with doing this with my own two hands.

It's not enough to just be there when Armand dies. I need to beat him. I need to see the light leave his eyes myself, and I need to be the cause of it.

My therapist shocked me by taking an interest in what he labeled my "revenge fantasies." He had me write them down in detail and talk about them with Uncle Bradley.

I was completely shocked when my uncle turned out to be all for the idea, and even more surprised when he decided to pay a group of investigators to find Rossini so that I could exact my revenge. Before all of this, my uncle always nagged me about being "more ladylike" when I always preferred to run, swim, and hike. But from the moment I brought up my dream of ending Rossini myself, he changed his tune completely.

I don't really know what I would have done without him.

But all the support, practice, and determination in the world can't change one hard reality: Rossini is very likely going to kick my ass tonight, or put a bullet in me. That's why I have requested gear that should help me either live long enough to kill him and get out, or take him with me.

Lightweight armored clothing in indigo, padded just enough to absorb some hits without making me sweat to death. Two long, sharp knives. The long rifle I got as a gift from Dad when I was twelve, and the heavy-caliber pistols I have practiced with for five years.

Just like with my martial arts practice, Bradley has no idea just how much time I've spent on the range in the last few years. He hired an instructor to accompany me before I hit age eighteen, but mostly stayed out of it. I don't know if he found the idea of my working out and shooting guns distasteful, or if he didn't actually care all that much how good I got at it.

That has never added up for me. He helps me, and then he neglects me. He reassures me that this revenge is what my father would want and spends a quarter million yearly looking for Rossini, but then sends me off on my own.

I start changing into my workout gear, and put on the light raincoat I will be wearing over it until I get to his mansion. Rossini doesn't keep any staff. No guards. No security system that I can't defeat even with my very basic skills. He's that confident in his ability to keep himself safe.

Either that or my uncle's got bad information. But the fact that he may have bad information is why I'm checking the place out tonight instead of just running in blindly.

I check my pistol. It's a Walther PPQ loaded with armor-piercing 40-caliber rounds. I've practiced with this same gun since I started my training; it's like an extension of my hand now.

My backup weapon is another Walther. I don't normally try for two-gun mojo with them. As my instructor is fond of telling me, those kinds of flashy stunts are just a way to miss faster, with more bullets.

My eyes narrow as I realize that the clip is loaded with blanks. "Very funny, courier man. Are you trying to get me killed?" I check my backup and find more blanks. Growling in irritation, I dig out one of the boxes of hollow points I ordered, make sure they are actually hollow points, and reload my clips.

I bag up the blanks while I fantasize about force-feeding them to the guy in the gray suit. *Damn unprofessional. I'm going to have to tell Bradley to find a better courier.* What would have happened if I had not checked?

Once I've loaded and holstered both weapons, tucking two spare clips into my belt pouch, I stomp into my boots and meet my own gaze in the mirror. I snort, rolling my eyes. *God, I look like I'm cosplaying.*

Even armed to the teeth and with a gun in my hand, I still look ridiculously young—like I'm sixteen instead of twenty. My uncertainty shows in my face, making my green eyes look innocent and vulnerable. I narrow them, and do my best to look tough.

"Time to get to work."

The light, opaque raincoat helps me blend in with the crowd going in and out of the lobby downstairs. I pass by people on the street outside without anyone noticing that I'm armed. No one would expect that of a young woman anyway—not around here.

I might die before this is over. But I've got a secret weapon in my small bag that will make sure that if I end up engaging with Rossini tonight, he won't be coming out of it alive. I hope I don't have to use it ... but if I do, it's a guaranteed win, so long as I can get within ten feet of him.

I weigh the small bag briefly in my hands before setting it carefully on the seat of my rental car and looping the seatbelt through its strap. It really wouldn't do to have such sensitive contents sliding off the edge of the seat.

I'm full of nerves as I start the drive out into the countryside, but they start to clear as I move further away from Atlanta. The warm rain and blustering wind fill the empty stretches of a nearly deserted highway. I chew mint gum to help keep myself alert.

Armand Rossini's hideaway is an hour away. I will get there and do as much as I can tonight. Whether it ends before dawn or I have to come back tomorrow, I'm not going to stop until it's done.

CHAPTER FIVE

Armand

I can't sleep. I'm too busy thinking about the innocent girl that has been wound up and sent after me. I have no doubt that my now-defunct client made sure to arm her as well. He's trying to force me to kill her in self-defense since I've refused to do it outright.

He's underestimated me greatly, along with my commitment to my code. My hands may be soaked in blood, but none of it is innocent. Mob bosses, serial killers, abusive husbands, sadistic fathers—those are my targets.

I'd rather take a bullet than kill Marina Shea—not just because of principle, but because of pride. My troublesome former client deserves the bullet for trying to force me to compromise myself. And for deciding that a work of art like her deserves to die.

There's only one thing I can think about doing to that gorgeous young vigilante, and it has nothing to do with my guilt or her vendetta. If only her schoolgirl crush on me endured despite her knowing that I killed her father. But, of course, even hoping that is perverse.

Still, the idea of seducing her lingers, like an itch I can't scratch.

I'm not worried about her getting to the plantation house without my knowing it. There is a winding half-mile road that runs up to my gate, and I've seeded the area with various sensors and cameras hidden in the trees.

The moment she shows up in the area, I'll have a good five to ten minutes before I even have to worry about her reaching the edge of my property. The land leading up to my property line is actually county land, which I sold off to them to put a buffer between me and the highway.

I am not worried about her sneaking up on me. I'm just worried about her, period. She's a pawn in a very ugly game being perpetrated by a pair of human devils, and I really have to make sure that she isn't sacrificed. I want her to get out of this alive ... and armed with the truth.

If she learns what really happened with her father, she'll find a better target for all that rage she's aiming at me. But how do I get her to listen?

I get up and make myself an Amaretto sour, and sip it in my library as I watch the road out the window. Not a single sign of headlights anywhere out there. It gives me a little time to plan.

By the time my security system chimes a warning I already have the lights off all over. I have the camera feeds routed to my tablet, which I've turned to the lowest brightness so the glow won't give me away.

I'm wearing my low-light goggles, but I do not have any of my weapons. No one dies tonight. I have no intention of even letting her see me until I'm close enough to disarm her.

I glimpse her headlights well down the access road. There are no street lights at all, so it's easy to see her coming. This particular window has no plants on the sill, and no window box outside. By the time anyone reaches the gate, I can have a sniper rifle set up and ready to fire on them from here.

Instead, I just boost the magnification on my goggles, focusing in tight on her windshield, and her face beyond. She looks nervous, determined, and still so very young.

I take my phone out and bring up her photo, smiling a little. She might hate me, and with good reason. But goddamn, she's cute.

I watch her get out of her car in the shadow of one of the big cypresses just outside the gate. She slings a small bag over her shoulder and puts on a pair of goggles much like my own. I watch curiously as she walks past the taller iron gate and instead heads for the spike-topped iron fence.

I'm not worried that she'll be able to get over it on her own. Poor little rich girl; she may have spent some time at the range, but she's hardly a professional entry wom—

I stare in shock as she throws her raincoat over the top of the spikes and clambers over the wet iron like a monkey, scrambling up quickly and flinging herself over like the devil's on her trail. *Holy shit.*

I really like this girl! I can't help but grin. Apparently the young lady is full of surprises. And she's clearly brave, too. It only makes me want her more.

And that brings my head back to the same question: how can I convince her that I did everyone a favor—including her—by putting her father in his grave?

I watch her progress across my lawn, keeping to the shadowy edges as much as she can, her movements stealthy and cautious. She's avoiding the cameras. She's a little more hesitant and clumsy than a pro, but she's been practicing—and she definitely has a lot of potential.

I decide to power off the security grid on the lower floor. I want to see if she can get inside. If she does, I'm going to take care of her myself instead of letting the alarms go off to alert the neighbors—and the police.

She reaches the code box outside my door and manages to hack it after a few tries, deactivating the door alarm. She picks the lock and the deadbolt, and then quietly steps inside.

I move out onto the landing to watch her as she creeps through the entryway and into the dining room. I catch whiffs of hotel shampoo and hand cream as she walks past the stairs. It's familiar.

Which Atlanta hotel uses rosewater-scented toiletries again?

I file the question away in case I have to track her later, and move silently down the stairs to start following her more closely. It's not difficult to stay out of her view; she's moving slowly and fairly quietly, but I can hear her labored breathing. She's scared.

Of course she is. She might be brave and skilled, but she's an amateur trying to avenge her dad, and she probably thinks of me as some kind of unstoppable monster. But sometimes fear makes people more dangerous—frightened people with firearms can kill without even meaning to. I'm careful to stay in her blind spots.

The closer I get to her, the harder my cock gets. The way she moves, the flash of her pale skin against that dark, richly scented hair, the curve of her hips in those high-tech combat pants. She wants to be a tough girl; wants to be my enemy. But my lust for her is growing so strong that I barely give a shit about the potential danger.

We have reached my cavernous living room, with its display cases of small statuary and fossils, its sprawling velvet couches and thick Persian carpet. I move a little closer to her, still dodging her line of sight and using the shadows and furniture of the room to break up my silhouette.

I'm trying to decide whether to speak first or jump her to get the gun away when she catches a glimpse of my reflection in the glass of the cabinet doors. She tenses, and I lunge forward as she spins around.

CHAPTER SIX

Marina

The entire house is dark, but warm, and smells like it's been inhabited recently. Faint whiffs of garlic bread and steak from the kitchen. Amaretto from the library. And everywhere, the faint smell of spicy cologne.

I'm careful. I do everything right that I can possibly think of. Checking my corners. Moving carefully and quietly through the building, checking every room in case he's sleeping in there ... or somehow waiting for me.

Where are you, you son of a bitch? Where did you get to and why are you making no noise at all? Maybe he's not here after all. That would be a break, in a way ... especially with my stomach jumping around like this.

I'm halfway through the living room when I catch sight of movement behind me, in the reflection of one of the glass-fronted display cases. I spin around—and don't even get a chance to pull the trigger.

He's a lot bigger than I remember—and faster than I ever dreamed. He's already blocked the slide with his hand. A second later, he twists the pistol out of my grip and sends it sailing across the room.

I roll back out of his reach and pull my backup pistol—and he moves like lightning again, darting forward and grabbing both my wrists. Next thing I know, he has me pinned against the wall.

He's wearing night-vision goggles too, and his expression is more amused than angry. That pisses me off enough to get over my shock and start fighting his grip, squirming and kicking. *Maybe I can get a wrist free—*

No good. He lifts me partway off my feet and raps my gun hand sharply against the wall. My backup pistol clatters to the floor and he kicks it behind him.

I refuse to cry out. Teeth gritted, I fight his grip, trying to get a knee up into his gut, his balls, something. His response is to wedge a knee between my thighs and pin me more firmly, his whole body pressing against mine, anchoring me to the wall.

A sharp jolt goes through me. I've never felt anything like it before. It's hot and electric, and the closer his body presses against mine, the more it cuts through my fear and distracts me from my anger.

What are you doing to me?

"That's quite enough," he states, far too calmly for the situation. "Stop squirming. You're not going to be able to break my grip, and I don't want to have to you hurt."

I want to spit in his face, but when I raise my head to look at him all I can see are those perfect full lips smiling faintly in the dim moonlight. My mouth dries up immediately. "Damn you, let me go!" I snap.

"What, so you can try to kill me?" His black amusement stings. I hate him—and I hate even more that I can feel my body tingling from his closeness, from his rich masculine scent in my nostrils.

"You've got no damn business complaining. You murdered my father! Did you think I would just let you get away with it?" It's stupid to yell when he's close enough to just snap my neck, but I can't stop fighting.

That small, amused smile dies. "Your father was a monster. The only reason that you don't realize that is because you can't remember what he did."

I freeze, my whole body going cold despite his hot, powerful body pinning mine. My mind immediately goes back to the strange dream, and my father's annoyance with me for being afraid of the basement. And for a moment ... I *wonder*.

I catch myself and a wave of disgust runs through me. What the hell am I thinking, believing this murderer over my own family, even for a moment?

"I don't know who hired you, or what kind of lies he handed you when he gave you your advance, but my father was a great man."

"Your father was under investigation by the FBI and the hospital board at the time of his death. If what he and his partner did had ever become public knowledge before he died, he would have died in prison." His tone has a note of pity to it, as if I'm some poor brainwashed creature who can't grasp the truth. "I am sorry that he has deceived you so badly, on top of everything else."

I just stare at him.

He switches both my wrists into the grip of one broad hand and pulls off both our night-vision goggles so that he can look me in the eyes. "I'm not saying these things to hurt you. You may not believe this, but I don't mean you any harm."

I can't help it; I burst out laughing. "You don't mean me any harm? You murdered my father! Don't you think that would hurt me at least a little?"

He lets out a sigh and his head lowers slightly. To my

complete surprise, his handsome face creases with pain. "I'm sorry. Whether he was a good man or not, I have taken him from you, and I deserve your anger. But when it comes to seeking revenge, there's someone who deserves your bullets far more than I."

I have no idea what to say. My heart is pounding; my breath burns in my lungs. He's apologizing to me. That's even crazier than hearing him say that my father deserved his fate. "Stop," I mumble finally.

He sets me back on my feet and moves back slightly, but his hands still hold my wrists like warm, smooth manacles. "Stop what?"

"Stop playing head games with me. I came here to get the name of the man who hired you, and then kill you. I'm not going to stop until one of us is dead. And you caught me. So stop toying with my mind and just get it over with!"

He's going to kill me. Of course, he is. That's what he does.

"Get what over with? Are you assuming that I plan to end your life?" There's that amusement again, this time with a hint of self-deprecation. "I'd really rather explain the situation, and see if we can work this out."

"Is that why you're pinning me against a wall?" I point out, and he snorts.

"As lovely as this position might be under much different circumstances," he replies in a deep, rumbling voice as his thumb slides briefly along the inside of my wrist, "I'm only pinning you against the wall to keep you from attacking me."

"Stop talking like you're innocent," I growl, trying again to kick him. "It's not like my attack is unprovoked. And as for the rest, you're just making up lies about my father to try and confuse me!"

"If that was my aim, I'd come up with something a lot smoother than pointing out that your father was being investigated when he died. However, you're welcome to dig for information on the case, if you wish. That won't exactly help our immediate situation, though."

Even if he's lying, I have trouble not listening to him. His voice is amazing. His accent turns his soft tones into rolling, lilting music, teasing at my ears and leaving me breathing faster.

I'm face to face with the man who killed my father, and not only have I failed to get revenge—I can't even stop wanting him. Tears of frustration fill my eyes. "Stop it. I know you can't let me live."

Suddenly, without any warning, he lets me go. He still stands close to me, and I know better than to go for the guns or the knives on my belt. Instead I rub my wrists while he sighs and shakes his head.

"My dear, you have known my name for five years. If that was really a concern to me, I would have paid you a visit a long time ago. But it is not. If I were you, I would be more concerned about the person who paid me to kill your father."

"Who was it?" I demand, and he smiles sadly.

"That's a fact that I don't think you're ready to deal with yet. You're in such denial about your father that you've forgotten him to protect your heart. If I give you the name of the man who wanted both of you dead, you'll just deny that too. You're not ready."

"You condescending bastard!" I lash out, slapping him hard across the face—so hard that my hand burns afterward. He takes it, rolling with the blow and then looking back at me calmly. His response shocks me into silence for a moment, and then I growl more quietly, "That's not your call. You don't even know me!"

"No, but sadly, I know the man who gave the order. He doesn't expect me to try and reason with you. He was hoping I would just shoot you, that you showing up here would just be one more reason among many to get rid of you."

"Just tell me who he is and why he wanted my dad dead." I have knives. I'm aware of their weight on my belt. I could yank one from its sheath and drive it into his belly.

Or rather, I could try. He was fast and skilled enough to strip me of my guns before I could get a shot off. What makes me think that I'll have any more luck with a blade?

"Your father had a partner in his criminal ventures. After a brush with his secret left you traumatized and his marriage destroyed, he tried to retire. His partner refused to let him walk away from the fortune they were making, and had him killed.

"I agreed to the job because one of the people your father killed was one of my local informants. I was pissed off. I should have taken a closer look at who was calling my shots." There's a slight pleading note in his voice, as if he's almost desperate to convince me.

My lips are going numb. I can see the basement door yawning open like a door to hell in my mind's eye. I just manage to mumble, "My father never killed anyone. He was a doctor. He *saved* lives."

"Burke and Hare didn't start out by killing either." He stares down at me ... and then shocks me by reaching out to tenderly brush my hair back behind my ear.

I shock myself even more by standing there and letting him. The warm brush of his hand against my cheek does more for me than a kiss ever has, making me even more conflicted than before.

"I think you should go," he says quietly. "Leave my home, and don't ever return with a weapon on you, or I'll take it personally. If you stay ... I will only add to the turmoil I can see in your eyes. Do the research. Verify what I am telling you. And answer this: who stands to benefit most financially from your father's death?"

"Me," I reply. "But I wouldn't be risking my neck trying to get Dad some justice if I was the one who had him killed."

"No, you would not. But you need to understand. Your father's partner had him killed in part for leaving their "business," in part for fear of being exposed, and in part because he had only one way left to make money off of your father—inheritance. Who else stands to inherit your father's billions if you are ... removed from the picture?"

The room lurches around me. "What are you saying?"

"I am saying that he tried to contract me for more than one hit, and I refused yours. Because I don't murder innocent young women, even if they come to my home with a gun."

He cups my chin, his grip gentle but firm. "Have a close look at your father's will, *cara mia*. Take a look at who stands to gain if you should die. Then you will truly understand why you were sent here."

CHAPTER SEVEN

Armand

After she flees without her guns, leaving me alone with my lust and turmoil, I watch her drive off down the road, going only a little too fast. *Marina. Cara mia, I am so sorry.*

I hate being the bearer of bad news.

I turn the upstairs lights back on, reset the security system, and go upstairs to my library again. I bring up my file on Marina and her family on my tablet and shake my head as I look over all the ugly details that I have not told her yet. She's braver and cleverer than expected, but I know she would never have believed me if I tried to explain the truth about her father's murder straight out.

It started out small, well before Marina was ever born, when both her father and his partner were department heads at the county hospital. It was decades before anyone started to catch on; the discrepancies between donor lists and harvested organs only came to light after a pair of discreet early retirements.

The black-market organ business is always hungry, and they pay well. Unauthorized organ harvesting from the recently deceased is easy if they have a donor card, and only a bit harder if they don't. But there are a limited number of corpses in a hospital.

That was when the partners started making their own. Using a hidden harvesting facility, they found a particularly hideous way of turning Denver's homeless population into pure profit. That poor girl and her mother lived their lives with a monster that Mengele would have been proud to work with, and neither one of them knew.

Eventually, her mother fled, and Marina has holes in her memories that she blogs about on social media. I think that they found out, and I think that neither of them could handle it—each of them reacting in different ways.

It took me some time after the initial contract to find out who the partner really was, and I've been determined to put a bullet in him ever since. Unfortunately, he's deliberately drawn Marina as close as possible, probably to control her. I know he will use her as a human shield if I close in.

Coward.

I've gotten enough information about Marina over the years to know that she won't be leaving town until this is resolved. She's waited five years for revenge. I'll have to be patient to see what happens when the facts I have given her finally sink in.

An hour later, one of my phone rings suddenly. It's the number I have kept around only for that singular client, who thinks he's anonymous.

I connect the call and snap, "What is it?" My tone is full of impatience.

"Is it finished? Is the girl dead?" He's so eager that he's hyperventilating.

I open my mouth to curse him out, threaten him, tell him that I know who he is and I'm coming for him. But I'm too smart to give him the warning.

"The girl never found me. The house outside Atlanta that you sent her to is currently unoccupied. I have a nice video of her breaking and entering, but I think I'll be keeping it to myself."

I hear him curse under his breath and bite back a laugh. "You can't hide forever. My man in Georgia will be watching for you."

"That's not a very bright idea, if he wants to live very long."

"What are you going to do, send me his heart in a box?" He mocks me.

"No, I don't think so. You'd probably try to sell it."

A long pause, and then the voice snarls, "Very funny. We're closing in on you, Rossini, no matter what you do. Either you complete the contract, or—"

"Or what?" I snap, voice sharp and hard. "You're going to call Interpol on me? You wouldn't dare. You know I would take you down with me."

There's a long pause as he splutters. For such a supposedly brilliant man, he's not very quick-witted. It's probably all the alcohol. "You're not the only professional in the business. I'm sure some of your competitors have grudges against you. If the girl can't do the job, I'll kill her myself and send one of them after you."

I feel my free hand clench into a fist so hard that my knuckles ache. He can threaten me all he wants—but when he speaks of killing that doe-eyed girl that he's already used so badly, I can't control my reaction. "She's an innocent."

"She's a liability. Your money is waiting in escrow for the *partial* completion of your assignment. Get it done, or things will go down just as I have insinuated." He hangs up abruptly, and I growl and shove my phone back into my pocket.

Marina. He aims to kill her if I don't do it. I have to warn her.

That means finding her hotel. The one with the fancy

toiletries that smell of rosewater. I've stayed there, entertaining a weekend fling. The lady came out of the shower with her skin smelling of the stuff three mornings in a row.

Praying I'm right, I walk into my expansive closet to put on a disguise. I'm still a wanted man—I can't just walk around letting my real face end up on security camera feeds.

I took away Marina's father. It's time that I make it up to her, even if that means protecting her from herself ... or her own flesh and blood.

CHAPTER EIGHT

Marina

By the time I make it back to the hotel, I'm exhausted. I've lost both my guns and almost all of my nerve. I still don't know why Rossini spared me. He could have shot me in the back before I ever realized he was there.

But instead he tried reason. He tried to explain what happened all those years ago. I don't know if he was playing some crazy mind game, or if he was telling the truth—or whatever he thinks the truth might be. He seemed so ... earnest.

I hit him as hard as I could and all he did was try to talk with me. He could have killed me with one punch. Instead I carry with me the memory of his gentle touch as he stroked my hair.

Who is this man?

I stare out the window of the hotel as I strip out of my clothes, letting everything drop to the floor—from my empty holsters to my underwear. My body aches and itches with unfamiliar sensations.

He confused me. He scared me. He said things with a straight face that sounded impossible, and insinuated even more. The man who hired him to kill my father also tried to hire him to kill me, to gain a clear shot at my father's money.

I'm sorry, Dad. I ran. I couldn't do anything. Tears of shame blur my vision as I stand naked in the darkened room. I go to cry in the shower for a while, but I'm so worn out that I just end up leaning against the wall while the water sluices over me.

I make sure the door is locked and then open the balcony door to let the smell of warm rain waft through the windscreen. I crawl into bed, squeezing my eyes shut and just wanting the world to go away for a while.

Someone is lying to me. The assassin I've been planning to murder for five long years, or Uncle Bradley. It might also be whoever is giving Bradley his information. Maybe he's being misled by my father's mysterious partner—if any part of what Armand said is true.

He was the one who encouraged me to verify what he was saying. Some of it I might be able to check into online. There's also one person that I know will have at least some answers for me. But I haven't talked to her in five years.

Mom. If Dad was a good man, why did you leave him? And if he wasn't, why did you leave me?

My hair is gathered into a damp ponytail, and I curl up under the sheet while the breeze from the rainstorm brushes against my cheeks.

I'm just dozing off when my phone rings. It's Uncle Bradley. *Damn it, leave me alone.* But the phone keeps ringing.

I finally pick it up, resentment stewing in my stomach. "Hello?"

"Any luck?" Bradley's voice sounds too cheerful, like he's forcing it.

I freeze. I can't possibly tell him what actually happened. "I searched the property. There was no one present. No car in the garage, no signs of recent activity, and the house was unheated."

The lies shame me further and I can feel my cheeks burn. I failed my family, and now I'm hiding the truth from them.

"Damn. Sounds like my lead wasn't any good after all. I'm sorry, sweetheart. You planning to come back home tomorrow?"

"No." I manage to make myself sound more determined. "Just because he was out tonight doesn't mean the lead wasn't good. All the other information that you gave me checked out. I'm going back tomorrow."

"Well, aren't you brave." Now he sounds genuinely pleased instead of the falsity from earlier ... but there's a condescending tone to it, as if he's talking to a dog. "Your father would be proud."

"Yeah." My father would be furious. So would Bradley, if he knew that the only reason I plan to stay in Atlanta is to figure out my next moves without his—or anyone's—influence. I already know that I can't kill Armand.

The whole time that he had me pinned against the wall, the explosives in my bag were within reach. I could have slipped a hand down into it when he let me go. I could have ended us both and avenged my father—it was what I had intended to do if I got caught. But I completely forgot about the damn thing until afterward.

He captivated me too much. His words confused me too much. And all it took was that unexpected seed of doubt to push any thoughts of a suicide bombing completely out of my head.

"All right, well, if my contacts in the area dig up anything else about him, I will let you know. Otherwise, call me when the job is done." Am I imagining the tiny edge to Bradley's voice as he finishes his sentence? *Hey, you fat old fart, if you want this done faster, come help!*

"Okay. Good night, Uncle Bradley."

I try to settle back into bed, but something about his voice in my ear has left me restless and unable to sleep. I get up, still naked, and go to my laptop, booting it up and connecting to the hotel Wi-Fi. The warm, moist breeze feels good on my skin. There's an exotic scent to it, and every now and then there's an undertone that reminds me of Armand's cologne.

It's too late to call my mother. The idea of trying to reach across the gulf between us makes me a little sick. I've never forgiven her for leaving, but she's the only person in the world that I absolutely know will not lie to protect my father—or my feelings.

With nothing else to do, I decide to take on Armand's challenge and start looking into my father's history. I never imagined that he was anything but an innocent victim of someone he managed to anger. And of course, I have few memories that contradict that, so I've always tried to assume the best.

Everything I can find online under my father's name talks about his medical achievements. His time as director of the hospital's surgical wing, his transition into medical equipment manufacturing ... and the death that the whole outside world believed was an accident. There's nothing here that I haven't read before.

Then, on a hunch, I run a search on the hospital where he worked. As soon as I alter the date range to search for stories from between five and ten years ago, news articles start popping up. Some of their headlines leave my hair standing on end.

Hospital morgue investigated for improper disposal of remains: former surgical director questioned over large number of body parts found in hazardous materials disposal after cremation chamber breaks down

Body parts in Denver hospital case match fingerprints from missing homeless vet, runaway teen

Suspected serial killer may have covertly disposed of victims' bodies in hospital medical waste

Former surgical director cleared of any involvement in medical disposal case; investigation shifts to morgue director and staff

I don't remember any of this. None of the news articles, no mention of the situation by my parents, nothing. But as I read the articles, my heart starts to beat faster, and that same terror that I feel in my nightmares starts haunting me.

Finally I drag myself to bed and take a tranquilizer just to force myself to rest. I'm trembling as I curl up under the covers. *Father, what were you hiding?*

I close my eyes. Falling asleep is a relief. What happens next ... isn't.

I don't know how I got myself wedged under my bed like a little kid or when I curled up there, still and silent. It must have been a while ago, because I'm getting stiff, and my body is sore from all the trembling I have been doing. Outside my bedroom, Mom and Dad are shouting at each other in a way I have never heard before.

"I found her on the floor of the basement. She's hiding under her bed, James! She won't come out and she won't talk! What the fuck is in that room down there, and why is it locked?"

"You should really calm down. She saw a few medical samples and got scared, that's all. She will be completely fine. Everything will be fine."

"Bullshit, James! She kept screaming about a freezer full of hands and feet!"

"Well, then, she's either psychotic, or hallucinating. Have you considered having her tested for drugs?" His voice sounds so reasonable—as if my mother is the crazy one. But the words that are calmly coming out of his mouth tell me a different story.

"Drugs? She's a good girl! She's never done drugs in her life! And she's got no history of mental problems, you know that."

"So why is she gibbering and crying under her bed, then?"

"That's what I've been asking you!"

The basement. Secrets locked down in the basement. A chest full of hands. Of feet. Of ... more. Anyone would have screamed.

"What have you done, James? What happened to our baby girl?"

I wake up cold and shaking, tears running like water down my cheeks and my chest burning as I fight back a scream. My heart beats so hard that my head throbs from it. My throat hurts; I know I must have screamed in my sleep.

Just a nightmare. It's not a flashback. It's not a memory. It is just a damned nightmare.

But deep down, I know better. All the confusion and horror that Armand left me with has percolated in my head. I suddenly have a clue as to why I was so terrified of that basement.

But was it just a misunderstanding? Maybe Dad had some pickled organs down there, like the kind you find in a biology classroom. Maybe I had a complete freak-out over nothing. Mom got mad, Dad got defensive, their relationship started to crumble. But if that was all it was, why can't I remember any of it?

I need to talk to Dr. Weiss, desperately. But it's the middle of the night and I know he won't be picking up. I'm totally alone; I don't know what to do; and the tears won't stop.

"Are you all right?"

The familiar soft voice comes from outside the screen. I look up in shock and see a shadow standing out there, tall and broad-shouldered. In that moment, I honestly wonder if I'm still dreaming.

Armand moves forward so I can see his face in the dim moonlight. He's dressed differently, his body swathed in a dark overcoat. A knitted cap fringed with fake blond hair hangs from one hand. Once again, no sign of a weapon.

I should be terrified. He's an experienced assassin, and he's right there; he could have shot me through the screen, or busted in while I was sleeping and finished the job with a pillow.

Instead, he's looking at me with worry from beyond the screen's boundary.

"What are you doing here?" I snap, suddenly realizing that I'm naked under the blanket. I clutch the fabric tighter around my body, cheeks burning.

"I am very sorry for the intrusion, Miss Marina, but there was no other choice. There have been some new developments, and the situation has become much less safe for you than before."

"Maybe because there's a fucking assassin on my balcony?" I snap, and he lets out a soft laugh.

"Touché. But, no, unfortunately. I mean that my former employer has upped the stakes against you, and you deserve to know the facts about it. For your own safety." He looks at the screen in front of him. "May I come in?"

"Fine, but I'm not coming over there." I don't want to let on that I'm bare-assed, and I certainly don't want to show him.

He shrugs. "Very well." One simple push in the right place and suddenly the screen lock doesn't work anymore. He slides the door open gently, steps in, and closes it behind him. "Is there any reason you are hiding in bed?"

My nipples tighten unconsciously, and I feel a rush of warmth flush through my skin. I *can* just show him, if I want to. Part of me—the part that has come to attention again now that I'm in his presence—would like that very much indeed. Probably, so would he.

I just don't have the nerve. "I just woke up from a hell of a dream. I'm not going anywhere for a minute."

His gaze holds mine as he crosses the room toward me. "Of course. What was your dream about?"

"The basement," I mumble, not wanting to get into detail. "The basement of my father's house. I found something down there when I was young. Something ... medical. It freaked me out so badly that I hid under my bed and listened to my parents fight for hours."

My eyes are stinging again, and I can't help feeling embarrassed. I don't want to start blubbering in front of this murderer. But my body and heart won't cooperate.

He settles onto the corner of the bed, his weight shifting mattress underneath us. "Are you sure that's all you found down there?"

The gentle question hurts like hell. I remember the bleak feeling of curling up all alone under my bed, my parents too occupied with arguing over me to comfort me. A sob tears its way out of my throat, leaving me hurting and humiliated as I bury my face in my hands.

"I don't know! There are pieces missing from my memories. I've been going to a hypnotherapist for years to try and get them back. But now I've gotten this one big piece, and it just makes everything else more confusing!"

I can't take it anymore. I have tried to keep my head clear and get the job done. But now, everything inside me is in chaos. "What did you do? How did you do this to me?"

"I gave you a piece of the truth. I'm sorry that it's so hard for you to process. But then again, there are reasons why your mind blocked out almost everything about your father."

"I still don't know who to believe, or who to trust." I'm shaking all over. But there's a growing feeling trying to edge out my pain. The awkward, tempting reality of being secretly naked in his presence is settling in. My mind must be casting about for a distraction.

Again, cowardly.

"Trust yourself, and trust the facts that you gather. Every other person in this world has an agenda, even if they care about you." His hand slides toward me across the top of the bedspread, and I shiver, wondering what will happen if this little secret is discovered.

"It's hard to trust myself when my memories are full of holes." I wonder how many horrors those holes contain. What did I block out, and why? Was my father actually a monster?

My father is a great man. I must avenge his death. My own life is not as important as making sure that the man who killed him pays.

The phrase rattles through my head as if it's being read off of a teleprompter. There's no emotion behind them, not love or anger. But they feel absolute, as if God himself handed them down.

"What the hell is happening to me?" I gasp, and burst into tears.

Then my world's foundation cracks again as he moves forward and pulls me into his arms.

CHAPTER NINE

Armand

I shouldn't be doing this. This vulnerable girl, however sexy and brave, should be off-limits to me. She is caught in the middle of a dangerous situation. I killed her father. I rode a wrecking ball through her whole world.

But I can't let her go.

I hold her lightly, giving her the opportunity to squirm away if she wants. But instead she buries her face against my shoulder. One hand grasps my shirtfront, clinging to me. The other is balled into a fist and smacks against my arm harmlessly.

As her tears soak through my shirt, the mix of guilt, empathy, and desire threatens to boil over inside of me. I stroke her hair gently, murmuring in a soothing tone that it will be all right, that she's strong enough to get through this, that I will help her.

When did her needs start mattering to me quite so much? I just came to give her a warning. I didn't come here to try and take her pain away.

But here she is in my arms, with my hand slipping over her silky hair and down to her shoulders. Which are ... bare. I blink. *Wait just a moment ...*

My fingers drift across her upper back stealthily, and then my arms settle around her again. On top of everything else, I'm suddenly forced to ignore a huge erection as I realize she must not be wearing anything underneath those sheets. *No wonder she didn't want to get out of bed. Oh my.*

Temptation gnaws at me. It's been too long since a woman has interested me this much. But she's upset and vulnerable, and I'm not that much of an ass. I shouldn't even be touching her.

But everyone in her life is a fucking Judas, from what I can tell. She has no one to treat her right. I might not be the right person for the job, but I still want to volunteer.

I bury my nose in her hair and hold her close, trying to ignore the mix of rose-scented hair and feminine musk that rises from her smooth, soft body. I can feel her breath catch and a tremor go through her as I hold her.

Her heartbeat is picking up. Her free arm stops flailing at me and wraps around me instead. I can feel her body relax against mine slightly, the soft globes of her breasts pushing against my chest.

Oh God.

When I idly hoped that her crush on me had never subsided, I certainly expected that it had. I never seriously considered what I would do if she still wanted me. But here she is, tears drying up as our bodies slowly become more aware of each other.

She looks up at me, her eyes searching my face. "Why didn't you kill me? Why are you helping me?"

If I'm feeling this confused by our inexplicable attraction, I can only imagine how she must feeling. She must be fishing for some reason for this to be okay, or at least for reassurance that her interest in me isn't one-sided. But I'm wary of her getting too attached—or maybe I'm worried about myself. Even as I continue to hang onto her and feel her palms slide up my sides, I know that will only make things worse for her.

Little Marina doesn't need a semi-retired assassin in her life. Nor does a twenty-year-old need a man who has started finding sprigs of silver hair mixed in at the base of his cock. So I'm quick to set her straight. "I'm helping myself."

"I don't understand." She sounds shyly disappointed, and my stomach tightens.

"If I can convince you of the truth, you'll stop trying to kill me, and I can get you off my back without killing you. Perhaps you'll even stop hating me. Maybe you'll move on with your life, and stop letting your family's past affect your future."

She just blinks at me, looking completely stunned.

I have to catch my breath. She feels so fucking good in my arms that I have to force myself to focus on anything other than the pleasure.

"As for not wanting to kill you, I tried to tell you. I have a code. I kill criminals and monsters. I don't touch innocents like you. But in this case, the man who wanted your father dead tried to send me after you. I refused, and so he orchestrated this meeting to try and force the issue."

She stiffens slightly in my arms, that hazy look of panic returning to her eyes. I don't know how bad her amnesia is, but I know that it's shielding her from terrible pain. My revelations from earlier helped to clear some of the fog in her memories, and that left her distraught ... and now I'm revealing even more.

I'm trying to be careful. She's traumatized enough without me making it worse. But right now, she's living in danger every day, and remaining ignorant will only make things more dangerous.

"You want revenge on this man because he ordered your father's death. I want revenge on him because he's trying to force my hand, and I absolutely will not allow him to force me for kill you. Once you've done your research and are satisfied that I am telling the truth, I propose that we hunt him together."

It's crazy enough that I'm not surprised when she lets out a shocked laugh.

"You're playing with my head," she chuckles incredulously. "You can't possibly expect me to just trust you. What about my revenge?"

"Damn it," I growl, cupping her face and staring intensely into her eyes. She freezes and her lips part, an unconscious offering. I force myself to ignore them.

"Shall I do penance, then? I can't help you get this guy if I'm dead, so you can't expect my life. Just tell me what you want from me and I will give it to you."

A shiver goes through her. Her hands slide up to grip my shoulders through my shirt. "Fine. If you're not fucking with me, here's what I want. You work for me now, until I'm done with you."

Her unexpected fire makes me ache. "Then ... what are your orders?"

"Tomorrow we can talk about this plan of yours. And for that I'll need the whole truth out of you, no matter how badly you think I'll react."

I hesitate, and then nod my agreement. "Done. What about tonight?"

She bites her lip and looks up at me softly. "Tonight, I need you to get all of this out of my mind. No more thinking about it. No more dreaming about it." She takes a deep breath and her eyes stray to my lips, so there's no mistaking her meaning. "Can you do that for me?"

My mouth goes dry. I swallow, and then give her my most charming smile. "I'm sure I'll come up with something."

CHAPTER TEN

Marina

I've never been one to do things halfway, and so it is with Armand.

His mouth captures mine hungrily, before I even have time to catch my breath. I've never asked for sex from anyone before. I never imagined that I could ... even in such a shy, indirect way.

Good thing that he understood me perfectly. And apparently, he's happy to help.

I've never been this close to an aroused man before. His eyes are bright; his muscles tighten and shiver a little as I run my hands over him. Now and again, the bulge running the length of his groin brushes against my lower belly.

The blanket still covers my breasts. Pinned between us as we explore each other's backs with our palms, it isn't going anywhere—yet. But his hands are sliding up and down my back, going lower each time ... until he grips my bare hips and caresses the globes of my ass.

I gasp into his mouth and hear him chuckle low in his throat before he kisses me even more fiercely. But the chuckle turns into a groan when I kiss him back with equal intensity, pressing my body against him boldly. I'm getting rid of my fear bit by bit, and all the lust and rage in the world is pouring in to replace it.

I hate you. I want you. Make up for what you did. Make me feel good, for once in my life.

He pulls me closer, his tongue flicking against mine, the breath from his nostrils hot on my cheek. The fabric of his clothes rustles maddeningly. I scratch him through his shirt, moving my hands between us to start unbuttoning it.

He lets out a surprised grunt but doesn't stop me, instead shucking the shirt off as soon as I have it unbuttoned and tossing it aside. His body is sleek and hard under his clothes, his olive skin smooth save for a few narrow scars, a thin trail of dark hair disappearing into the top of his trousers.

I run my nails over his skin, seize him, pull his hair, do my best to bruise his lips with mine. Everything I do seems to turn him on more. I don't know if I'm winning or losing.

I hear two thumps as he kicks off his shoes, and then he climbs further onto the bed with me, his eyes burning with desire. I've never seen a man look at me like this, with a mixture of worship and hunger. I lie back against the pillows, the blanket slipping partway off my breasts, and he crouches over me to kiss me again.

My hands trail over the skin of his back and then around to his belly, tugging lightly at his belt and sliding my fingers inside the top edge of his trousers. He sucks air as I unbuckle him and ease his zipper down. From his little groan of relief, he needed the extra room.

Do I really know what I'm getting into here? Do I really want my first time to be with him?

Tiny doubts keep trying to nibble at me but I push them away furiously. I hate that there's never been anyone else but him. I hate that only he has been able to turn me on this much.

I don't care if it hurts. I don't care if I wake up tomorrow and regret everything. This is an itch that needs to be scratched.

His hands slide all over my back, over my ass, my thighs, up my neck and into my hair. He grips my hair by the roots and tilts my head back so he can mark me with his mouth, the hard suction and little nips sending electric shocks through me.

Toes curling hard, I make a decision, and tug the blanket down off my breasts and belly.

He lifts his head and his eyes widen slightly. His free hand goes to my breast at once, squeezing it firmly and tweaking the nipple between two fingers. His mouth nuzzles its way up to capture mine again.

I whimper into his mouth and yank the rest of the blanket aside, needing to feel his skin against mine—from my lips to my toes. He wraps his arm around the small of my back, pulling me closer. I rub my breasts against his bare chest, the contact and his shudder of pleasure heating me up even more.

He lifts me to his mouth, running his lips over my throat and collarbones, then down between my breasts. I sigh, clinging to him, my head falling back limply as I push my breasts toward his face. His hot breath bathes my chest; my nipples tighten painfully as I hang onto him and murmur encouragement.

His mouth roams over my breasts, licking and kissing, inching slowly toward my aching nipples. I grip his hair, gasping and asking for more, and he obeys, swirling his tongue over one of my breasts before sucking my nipple into his mouth.

"Aah!" My back arches, more pleasure than I have ever felt leaving me squirming in his grip. He holds me firmly as I writhe, his mouth merciless as he pushes my nerves toward overload.

I hear my voice rising and falling with every long suck, moans of pure sensual bliss that I can't keep quiet. My hips lift with each one, grinding against his groin by reflex and making him shiver. I realize, astonished, that he wants me just as much as I want him.

He sucks my nipples until they're sore, leaves love bites on the undersides of my breasts, and then works his way downward, teeth and tongue teasing their way over my skin. He kisses my belly, nibbling at the edge of my belly button and then trailing downward as my eyes go wide in anticipation.

He grips my legs and parts them further, and I feel his warm breath blow over the trimmed hairs of my aching cunt. I freeze, craving pleasure but wondering again if I can handle this much. I force myself to stay still and let him work; he bends down and starts nuzzling and kissing me.

My back arches and my eyes roll closed as he parts my pussy lips. He kisses my folds, exploring them with his tongue, and I whimper, nails digging into my palms. Then he starts licking me with long lazy strokes.

"Oh ... oh *God* ..." I dig my nails into his shoulders as he laps gradually faster, each stroke of his tongue feeling better than the last. My head swims. My body has taken over, and when he starts swirling his tongue over my clit all I can do is react—and beg for more.

My hips roll with each lash of his tongue. My blood heats and tingles, and the longer he keeps working me over, the more my muscles tighten.

I dig my heels into the mattress and push myself up, craving climax ... but I can't get there. Not quite. I need to be *filled*.

"I need ... I ... *Fuck me!* I need your cock!"

He stops after a last few slow licks and looks up at me, smirking slightly. "Patience, *cara mia*."

"To hell with patience," I gasp out. I see the pleased glaze in his eyes ... which then catches fire.

He sits up and shoves his trousers and briefs down in one move, and I look down to drink him in. *Holy shit.*

It's my first time—not that I'm going to tell him that. I don't want him to feel honored, like he's special to me in any way. I'm scratching an itch. But I wasn't expecting to use such a big tool.

He reaches into his pocket before stepping out of his trousers, and I see a condom packet. *Cheeky fucker came prepared.* It amuses me more than anything—he said he came here to give me important information, but it seems he's been having fantasies of his own.

I watch him roll the condom over his huge, gleaming cock, a hazy sense of disappointment filling my addled head. I want to feel skin on skin—but there are some risks even I'm not willing to take. And apparently, he feels the same.

Considerate. Not exactly a remorseless killing machine, is he? Not what I expected at all.

"Don't be nervous," he purrs as he climbs back up to crouch over me. "I'm not going to hurt you."

I close my eyes to concentrate on the sensations as he slides the head of his cock into me. It goes in smoothly for the first inch, and he pants lightly, a long shudder going through us both. Then he seizes my hips and pushes in further, a long growl of pleasure slipping through his teeth.

Like a lot of girls, I was brought up to expect pain my first time. Torn hymens and blood. But instead, as he drags me by my hips onto his bent knees and grinds his cock into me another few inches, it's anything but traumatic. No pain, no blood; I'm so hungry to be filled by him that I would barely have cared, but it's still a surprise.

Being stretched open hurts a little, but it's a good pain, and only turns me on more. I squirm, wrapping my legs around his lower back to pull myself onto him further. I brace my arms behind me and arch my back, and he lets out a melodious groan and starts to thrust.

He steadies me with one hand on the small of my back. The

other settles onto my pussy and gently fingers my lips open just above where he's driving his shaft into me. He dips two fingers in ... then starts curling them against my clit in time with his thrusts.

"Aah!" I arch my back higher, feeling my breasts bouncing with his every movement as my pleasure starts intensifying again. His hand on my back slides up, lifting me a little to start roughly sucking my nipple.

My body takes over again, writhing and shimmying around his cock like I was made to have him inside me. He grunts with pleasure and holds still, letting me dance over him while he stimulates me. I can hear my little yelps and gasps turn into cries as my cunt tightens around his shaft almost painfully. It's less intense than his tongue on my clit, and yet now he's really rubbing me in all the right places.

My nails dig into his shoulders as I ride him harder and harder. One of my hands slides up into his thick curls again and I press my breast against his face encouragingly. His fingers and tongue never tire. When I start to tremble, they both speed up.

The burning in my thighs as I grind on him with all my strength fades into the background as an expanding fireball of pleasure gathers in my cunt. My arms tighten around him. His mouth slips off my breast and he groans hoarsely into my cleavage. *"Marina ..."*

The desperate, drugged worship in his voice sets me off as much as his relentless hands and powerful cock. Ecstasy explodes inside me, rushing through me in uncontrollable waves. I probably scream. I can't even tell.

He stiffens as I thrash against him, groaning with joy. My nails are embedded into the skin of his back but he doesn't even seem to notice. For a moment I think he's done, just like me. But then his dark eyes open, piercing into me, and I know from the heat in them that he's not done with me at all.

CHAPTER ELEVEN

Armand

Don't get involved. That's another part of my code. But unlike most other rules, this one's in there to protect me, not others.

I like women. I like sex. I love moments like this, when I'm buried up to the root in a woman's softness, nerve-endings tingling with fresh pleasure every time I draw out and sink back into her.

I want to cum, but I have more work to do first. Pinned under me, her hips rolling in response every time I thrust into her heat, Marina still has the strength to move.

I really need to fix that before I give in to my own pleasure. It's a matter of pride.

Her warm flesh welcomes me as I work over her, the mattress bouncing her body up against mine. Sometimes, we grind against each other, our rough fucking made smoother by her juices. Sometimes, I hold her down, thrust deep into her, and massage her clit until she leaves fresh scratches on my back.

When she gets close to climax I have to hold still; those rich hips and the tight muscles of her pussy start milking me so hard it's a fight not to blast off with her. Her wails of pleasure and sobs for more just make it that much harder.

Holding off my orgasm makes for the sweetest agony. It's so much better than I had even fantasized about. The strange desire between us burns so bright that I want to know if it might last forever.

Her cunt contracts around me again and her hips start that delicious shimmy again. I hear a man's harsh shouts mix with her low, exhausted sobs, and realize that they are mine.

"Oh, Armand," she purrs as she comes down—and that sexy little croon busts the dam inside me.

I throw myself over her, pounding into her hard, no longer able to restrain myself. She gasps and hangs on for dear life—and the friction alone starts her own muscles tightening again. Drunk on pleasure, I hear her cries of joy a final time.

Then my back arches, and my cock spasms inside of her. Each blast of cum roars out of me harder than I have ever experienced in my life. It takes all I have to silence my scream.

When the storm passes, I settle over her, feeling her arms wrap limply around my shoulders. We lie there entwined, floating on a cloud of soft contentment, and I lay my head on her shoulder.

I'll just rest here for a few minutes, I think, too blissed out and infatuated with this adorable woman to want to leave her bed just yet. *Just for a little while.*

She starts stroking my hair, and I close my eyes.

CHAPTER TWELVE

Marina

I know I'm not supposed to be down here in the basement. Daddy's rules. The only thing I'm ever allowed to do is take the immediate left at the bottom of the stairs into the wine room so that I can fetch him a bottle or three.

It seems to amuse him to send me down to a place where stepping through the wrong door could get me grounded for a week. It amuses him more that my mother hates this habit. "She's fifteen and you're treating her like your sommelier, James. What are you thinking?"

Daddy is a prick. Nobody in my family would be surprised to hear that. But I'm the only one who actually says it.

Sometimes I have a problem filtering the things that come out of my mouth—as my current grounding proves once again. One of my friends from self-defense class is a boy, and suddenly Dad's interrogating me about poor Jamie left and right, being all nosy about our relationship.

I finally pop out with the truth. "Damn it, Dad, Jamie is gay as hell. We're not dating, let alone screwing, so you can stop talking to me about how boys will ruin my life."

Somehow this is disrespectful enough that he grounds me for a week—for setting him straight on his worries. So I figure, if he wants to punish me, it may as well be for something that is actually worth it.

The basement of our old house has sprawling rooms, some of them made of ancient brick and stone, others of plain concrete. Most of them are being used for storage.

But there's a door in the back that is firmly closed—though right now its padlock hangs open.

We used to have underground parking beneath the house, but when I was twelve—around the time that Dad retired—they walled this section of the basement off. The garage entrance still opens onto the road that runs along the back of the property, but until now, I always thought it was sealed as well.

Now, as I open the door and my flashlight gleams off of clean stainless steel and tile, I'm not so sure. The former garage is still in use. But instead of housing cars, it's full of medical equipment.

There are five of what look to be chest freezers lining one wall, with temperature monitors attached. The other walls are lined with every shape and size of stainless-steel cabinets. I grab the handle of one that looks like an oven door and it rolls out ... and out.

It's a morgue drawer. What the hell?

I move further into the room, and a drain grate rattles as I step on it by accident. The sloped floor is faintly stained with dark streaks, and there's a strong smell of bleach. My flashlight slides past an unmarked white delivery van that sits at the base of the garage ramp, and falls on something even weirder.

Dad's a surgeon. I know what a surgical theater looks like—and I am definitely looking at one right now. But why is it in our basement?

There's a large, ordinary chest freezer here, with a clear lid. I walk over to it, my stomach doing flips. Why would my father be doing secret surgeries in our basement?

I shine my light down into the fridge, and what I see there sends a flash of horror through me that knocks my thoughts into chaos. I remember dropping the flashlight. I remember running for the stairs. I *remember my legs giving out before I can reach them, my knees hitting the floor.*

Everything becomes a blur. My mother, calling my name in a panic. My father sighing in exasperation and then speaking to someone else.

"She's seen too much. But she's my daughter. What do we do?"

I hear loud knocking from somewhere, pulling me from sleep. But before the dream dissolves I hear a familiar voice say, "I know a specialist. Leave it to me."

I sit up naked in my tangled bedclothes and realize that I am alone—Armand has vanished. Someone is banging on the door so loudly that I worry it might be the police.

The rich scent of sex and expensive cologne clings to me as I wrap the sheet around myself and get off the bed. My legs are wobbly, the insides of my thighs sore. Yet despite the rude awakening, my body is more relaxed than I can ever remember it being.

Under my disorientation and annoyance at being awakened by whoever is still making a racket at my door, I feel a stab of disappointment that Armand has made himself scarce. But it makes sense—being caught naked with me would cause trouble for us both.

"Who the hell is it?" I manage, the horror from the dream sending jolts of adrenaline through me. I lean against the wall halfway to the door, clutching the sheet to my chest, the room lurching around me.

"Miss Shea? Are you all right?" The voice is a light tenor, touched with a Georgia twang. "My name's Corbett Chang. I work for your uncle."

I look around at the rumpled bed, my scattered clothes everywhere, my tangled, wild hair, my semi-nude body showing slight bruises in the mirror from Armand's fingers. There's no hiding that I had a man here last night. Especially if this guy is an investigator Uncle Bradley has hired.

"I'm fine. If you have news for me, I'll meet you down in the hotel diner in twenty minutes," I shout through the door, still leaning against the wall.

"I'll wait out here," he says cheerfully, and I curse under my breath.

I take my time showering, leaving the window open to air out the room. It's pouring outside—warm, misty rain, such a contrast to Colorado.

I keep my mind off the nightmare, thinking instead of anything else. What to tell the damn investigator. What clothes I have that will cover the suck marks on my neck and the backs of my thighs.

Armand's words. Armand's body. Armand's groans of ecstasy in my ear.

He said I was in danger. He promised to explain everything. But then the idiot outside showed up, forcing him to take off without so much as leaving his phone number. *Damn it.*

I just gave my virginity to my father's murderer. I should be ashamed of myself. But instead there's this bitter, ugly, rebellious pride welling up inside of me that I can't quite understand. How can I enjoy such a slap in my father's face?

It's got to be a chemical reaction. The sex itself was amazing —liberating. It left me hungry for more, and after last night, I'm confident that I can get it. Even that horrible dream—the details of which are slowly coming back to me as I wash and dress— can't rob me of this afterglow. It must be endorphins or something.

I throw on some plain jeans and a T-shirt under my tobacco-colored leather jacket. Just a ponytail, almost no makeup. My knives are barely visible on my belt.

I'm trying to avoid looking freshly fucked. I've even made the bed.

But now this creeping, cold feeling is welling up inside of me. My dreams tend to fade away once I wake up. But sometimes—and this only happens with the nightmares—they actually get clearer and more detailed once the fog of sleep wears off.

This is crazy. Once I get this meeting with Chang over with I'm going straight back to Armand's for some damn answers. And maybe a second round of sex—but only once he helps me figure out what the hell is going on in my head!

Chang's knocking again. "Miss Shea?"

"Yeah." I walk to the door, shoes still off, and let him in, not even trying to hide my annoyance. "What's this about?"

The man on the other side of the door is Chinese, about medium height, tanned and muscular, with a winning smile that looks forced. He's in a pale linen suit a few shades lighter than my jacket. His hair is swept back and streaked with brown, and his eyes flick over me alertly. "I'm sorry for the inconvenience, but this should be discussed in private. May I come in?"

"Fine." I step back and he walks past me, looking around. I shut the door. "So state your business. You woke me up from some badly needed sleep."

Actually I badly needed to wake up from that awful dream. I just wish I had forgotten it in the process. But instead, it's coming into horrible focus.

"Your uncle asked that I watch out for you while you're in Atlanta. A strange man was spotted on your balcony late at night. My contact on staff was slow in getting the information. I was going to dismiss it, but then he overheard screaming a few minutes before I came knocking."

I eye him. "You're telling me that you had me spied on, noticed that I had a visitor, but only came running because I screamed—in my sleep?"

His smile fades into a slightly sheepish look. "Uh ... okay, well, obviously this is a big misunderstanding. And it's your uncle who has people spying on you, not me, and it's to look after your welfare."

"Sure it is." *He's making sure I actually finish the job—finish Armand.*

Well, fuck him, he's got no proof I'm lying. I know no one could have followed me onto the property at Armand's place, so no one could have spied on our interaction. *For all anyone knows, the house was empty when I got there, just like I told Bradley.*

There's more of that resentment filling me up as I stare back at this man who was hired by my uncle. "I had a visitor last night. You know how hard it is to have privacy when you live with your damn uncle? And you will be so fired if he discovers that you were spying on me having sex."

He actually blushes. He might be a scumbag private investigator and my uncle's spy, but it's almost cute. "I'm not going to say a damn thing to him about that. But why were you screaming?"

"I have nightmares. Bad ones." I rub my temple. The cold feeling is spreading up from the pit of my belly, and the room feels like it's lurching a little with each heartbeat.

"What kind of nightmares make someone scream like that?"

The basement. The secret surgery. The white van. The freezer.

Suddenly I have to grab the wall. My heartbeat pounds in my ears. A whimper of panic escapes my throat.

"Miss Shea? Are you all right?"

It's not a nightmare.

"Dr. Weiss. I have to talk to Dr. Weiss!"

It's the last coherent thing I say before my knees hit the floor. Hard, cold memory floods my head.

The freezer. The face in the freezer. The face without eyes.

CHAPTER THIRTEEN

Armand

Walking outside in Denver in March is like walking into a fucking freezer. I pull my wool topcoat closer around my body, despising the wind that cuts right through it the moment I leave the airport. But after four weeks of waiting and no damn word, I have to go after Marina.

It's risky for both of us, me chasing after her. Her uncle is having her watched at all times, as I discovered the night we made love. I know I won't be able to get near her house. I'll have to tail her without being seen, and I know that finding an opportunity to reach out to her undetected will take time.

I'm just glad I came to her hotel in disguise; otherwise they'd have known that I visited her without killing her. If they knew that, they might consider *her* suspect, and I can't let that happen.

Two disasters happened the night of the best sex of my life, and I have to talk to Marina about both of them. But the man who came banging on the hotel room door, forcing me to sneak out via the balcony, drove her to the airport almost immediately. And now I have to find a way to reach her.

I discovered our first problem on my way to shower that morning. That adorable minx knocked me out with the rubber still on. I woke up wondering if I would have to hunt for it in the bedding, but no. I felt the bottom band squeezing me a little as I walked to the bathroom.

Then I flicked on the light—and discovered the condom hanging in rags from my cock. Complete blowout—I fucked my way right through it in my enthusiasm. *Damn.*

Telling her is a formality I always follow with my lovers. I'm clean; my last comprehensive STD test was two weeks ago. And it's not like I could get her pregnant even if I wanted to. But I really should let her know, just as a courtesy.

The second part, though, is a lot more important—life and death, even. Because if I don't fix things, there will definitely be consequences for her. And she's suffered enough.

The interruption that morning prevented me from giving her the whole story about the hit on her father, including the name of her father's partner. But from the way she screamed in her sleep that morning, I have a feeling she's already remembering things.

I don't know how much she witnessed of that whole horrible business. I know from my research that she's been in therapy ever since, and I hope it has helped her. But it doesn't seem like it has. How is it that she can't remember anything about her father still, even after five years?

Maybe it's just that horrible. I couldn't wake her up from whatever that nightmare was that morning in the hotel. I held her and shook her and tried to soothe her, but all she did was cry and struggle, and mumble something about a basement.

That's the third reason I'm here. I don't know how safe she is, staying in that place with her father's partner.

I get myself settled in a nice hotel room and turn the heat in the suite up the moment I close the door. I have two matching sky-blue suitcases with me, one of which was slipped onto the carousel for me by a black-market courier whose day job is in baggage claim.

You can't get weapons and gear through an airport these days. Specialized couriers have gotten rich off of increased security, and it is still easy enough to get what I need through customs.

I have two plans as I draw the shades and then lay open the second suitcase on the bed. I use the bug finder to sweep the room, and thankfully find nothing. Then I pull my gear belt out, and look at the array of pistols beneath.

I have both of Marina's Walthers with me. I imagine she will want them back. In the meantime, I holster them both, one under my arm and one at the small of my back. My stiletto goes up my sleeve. I felt naked without my weapons while I traveled —I've felt that way anytime I've been unarmed since I was fifteen—and now I relax a little.

My sources tell me that Marina has therapy tomorrow morning at 10 in Denver, and that she usually decompresses by taking a walk in the park adjacent to her therapist's office. I will do my best to meet her there without any of her uncle's men noticing.

Meanwhile, the very thought of Marina has me horny, and since I can't look her up, I look up some local wine bars and think about braving the cold. I'll find some thirsty, oblivious local girl and seduce her, and try to stop brooding about the one I'm here to save.

I'll probably be thinking of her the whole time, no matter what I do. What we had that night went beyond the sex. Waking up in her arms soothed something deep inside of me. Even as I steer my rental back onto the road with the wine bar's address on my GPS, I want that feeling of peace again.

I don't realize how badly I've been craving it until I pull up in front of Marina's therapist's office instead of the bar. "Shit," I mutter, starting to get worried about the effect she's having on me. I'm never this careless.

But that doesn't change the fact that I need to talk to her.

Breaking into Dr. Weiss's office is painfully simple. He's forgotten to set any kind of lock or alarm on his third-floor window. Of course, an ordinary man couldn't make the leap onto his tiny balcony from the car park rooftop. But I have been training longer than most parkourists have been alive.

I'm in quickly enough, my gloved hands leaving no prints as I slip inside, close the window, and start looking around for her file using my night-vision goggles. I'd give more of a fuck about invading Marina's privacy if I wasn't here to save her life.

Getting her number and talking to her tonight are all I'm thinking about. I want her to live. And, if I'm being honest with myself, I just want to talk to her again.

I'm not supposed to get attached. But that does not mean that I haven't.

I end up having to do a brute-force search to get the password for the ten-year-old desktop computer on the reception desk, but that doesn't take more than ten minutes. Despite the aging equipment, every file is neatly copied online. It includes everything—phone numbers, addresses, diagnoses, case and session notes.

When I find Marina's, I hesitate. I write down her phone number, but after that I stop and wonder if I should be looking. Maybe if I know more about what she is going through, I can figure out how to help her.

Her mother lives in and around Europe, jet-setting on widow's money—her divorce wasn't final when James died. I take down her contact information as well. I wonder if Marina has tried to speak with her since leaving me that morning. She was so distraught that I wonder if she's ready to handle it yet, no matter how desperate she might be for information.

But we're running out of time. *I'm sorry, cara mia, I must be a bit of a nosy bastard if I am to do right by you.*

I open up her file notes:

Diagnoses: Post-Traumatic Stress Disorder, non-complex, dissociative amnesia complicated by delusions

Notes: Patient presents with dissociative amnesia as a primary disorder, comorbid with PTSD. Both disorders appear to stem from a traumatic event of unknown origin that occurred in the basement of her family home. Her father, James Shea, referred her upon hospital release.

I sit back. *Wait a moment.* She told me that her therapist told her that her amnesia came from trauma from her father's death. But if her father referred her well before then …? So why was she told one story, when there's a whole different one written down on the page? I read on:

Initial attempts to unearth her lost memories through hypnotic regression and talk therapy seemed to lead to breakthroughs. However, the "memories" she unearthed appear to be a persistent delusion covering for some unknown and very real trauma.

The delusion, although consistent, is thoroughly false, as it describes impossible activities in a nonexistent location. Patient's delusion consists of falsely believing that her father was involved in criminal activity and was killed by a dashing vigilante. The idea is too far-fetched to be worth investigating.

I let out a little laugh. "Dashing vigilante? Is that what you whispered into your pillow at night when you started remembering things, you little devil?"

Well. Then that is what I'll become. I'm rich enough to stop working for money, and we made a deal that I work for her now, until she releases me. And that's just what I'll tell her if she asks why I'm here.

I steel myself to keep reading, but there's too much. I download the file onto a thumb drive and take it with me instead. Once I have a look, it'll be time to make some calls.

CHAPTER FOURTEEN

Marina

My period is late, and I wake up sick to my stomach. Has it been four weeks since my encounter at that Atlanta hotel? I lost track of time for a while, as Dr. Weiss was helping me put my head back together.

I check my calendar. Yes, I flew out to Atlanta just under a month ago. I had my period a few days before that, so ... these symptoms are definitely not good signs.

Fuck.

Anne, our cook, makes me a lean breakfast of chicken sausage, scrambled eggs, and strawberries. The sausage tastes too greasy, the eggs taste like they're dripping with butter. I nibble on a few berries and try to ignore the smell of everything else.

Anne is sixty-four and never misses a damn thing. She squints at me, her wrinkled face pulling into a shrewd little frown. "You pregnant, girl? Your uncle will kill you."

I can't keep the shake out of my voice. "My uncle needs to mind his own damn business. I'm twenty."

"Fine then, I'll mind your business. You go to the doctor?"

"I'll go tomorrow, before therapy." I'm not sure I'm comfortable that anyone else even suspects. "It's pretty scary to think about."

She shrugs. "You like the guy?"

I close my eyes, and my mind slips back to the man I still can't get out of my head, and the one night I had with him. His hands, his body, his mouth—his cock moving tirelessly inside of me as I came again and again. I can't even sleep without thinking about it and trying to touch myself the way he did.

I can bring myself off and enjoy it silently in my lonely bed, but it's a tiny, watered-down thing compared to what I felt that night. "He was worth the risk," I say simply, and she nods.

"Good. Either way you go, at least he wasn't some idiot. There are few things more regrettable than riding the wrong dick."

I burst out laughing, breaking the tension. "Damn, Anne!"

"It's true, though." She squints at me again. "You feeling okay? You were a real mess when they brought you back home."

I wince. "Don't remind me." It was so humiliating to have another breakdown. Now, I don't even remember what I was screaming about in Dr. Weiss's office the day that I got back.

I wouldn't know what caused it, either, if I hadn't feverishly written part of it down in my diary right before my emergency therapy session. I don't even remember doing it, but I found it as soon as I came home:

There were body parts in the basement. Dad was doing something down there. I looked up Burke and Hare after Armand brought them up. They stole bodies from the graveyard and sold them to artists and scientists for dissection. But the money was so good that they started killing people and selling their corpses.

Don't forget this time. Don't forget!

But I forgot dream, and I was glad. It was all a delusion. We didn't actually know yet what had happened in that basement.

Still, I kept the note, and kept it hidden. I don't know why; maybe it fascinated me. It's like a secret message from another me.

"I feel better. But now I have to track down the guy I was with that night, and that's going to be difficult." I am afraid I'll become unstable again if I go back to Atlanta. Uncle Bradley's right, it's best that I stay here.

"You'll manage. You still having those dreams?"

I fake a smile. "Sometimes." It's still every night.

"Hmph. You still scared of the basement too?" She lets out another grunt as I flinch slightly and drop my fork. "That's a yes. Girl, there is nothing down there! You need to go down. Face your fear. You'll feel better once you do."

Anne means well, and I give her a smile. "I'm working on that."

"Work harder," she instructs. "Life is short."

I wish I could.

I spend the day doing my usual routine—a jog, light training in my room, and a bit of meditation to try to sort out my memories. I understand that my mind made up a bizarre story to cover up the facts, and that I will need to figure out what is behind them. But the note in my diary, coupled with my possible pregnancy, isn't leaving me with much headspace today.

I'm settling in for the night when my phone rings. Unknown number. I pick up. "Hi, who's this?"

"Are you alone?" Armand's voice is low and urgent.

I gasp.

"Don't hang up." While I try to form some coherent words, he goes on. "I know you're being watched. I need to see you in private. It's urgent."

Well, speak of the devil. "Yeah, we should definitely talk. But I can't get out without being seen."

"Fine, then please hear me out. I'm guessing you never told anyone about our encounters together."

"The talking, the fighting, or the fucking?" My voice breaks a little. My stomach is jumping around even worse.

"All of the above."

"No, of course not." I keep my voice low. "So what is it?"

"Meet with me tomorrow in the park after your therapy session. I will wait for you there," he urges.

"Look, I had a breakdown the last time we met in person. Maybe we should stick to the phone for now." I want to see him, though—so badly that I can taste it.

"I am very sorry if I contributed to any trauma that the return of your memories may have caused. It was not my intent. I was only trying to explain the situation, and warn you of the danger."

"What you did was feed into my delusions," I snap. "My father wasn't some kind of body snatcher! It took my therapist weeks to help me get rid of those false memories!"

There's a long pause. "False memories? Are you saying that he gets rid of your memories?"

I frown, puzzled. "No, he helps me sort out which memories are true, and which ones are delusions."

"Marina," he says in a tone of deep worry, "those aren't delusions."

"That's ridiculous. Why would my therapist—" I can't even finish the thought before another wave of nausea hits me and I have to stop talking just to catch my breath. *Ugh, no, no, not now.*

"Are you all right?"

I have to tell him. "No, I very likely have morning sickness. So, thanks for that too."

An even longer silence, then he speaks breathlessly. "What?"

"I'm going to the doctor tomorrow." My heart's beating so hard that I have to listen around it.

"I ... have you had any other lovers lately?"

"Never in my life," I snap defensively, before realizing what I just said and blushing down to my goddamn toes.

That just seems to stun him more. "Never? Before me?"

"No," I growl into the phone, half angry and half desperate. "I've never even wanted anyone else. Not since the first time I saw you, you bastard. Even knowing that you killed Dad.

"I came up with this whole false reality after Dad died—that he was a bad guy and you were saving me from him. All that just to try to justify a giant, stupid crush I have on my father's murderer—on you! That's a secret I hide even from my goddamn therapist. You've got me all messed up in the head!" Tears spring to my eyes. I know I shouldn't be saying this—this is the first time I've ever even put all of this into words—but it's all just too much. It's all I can do to keep my voice down.

"*Cara* ..." he murmurs, and I let out a small sob.

"Now you've put a baby in me. How am I supposed to hide that from my family?" I'm shaking.

"Come with me," he replies very softly.

"What?"

"Leave that place. Come away with me. Bear the child. Even if you don't wish to stay, even if you don't wish to be a mother, leave the child with me. You'll be free of your family, and I'll give you anything you want."

I have no idea what to say. He takes a shivery breath, and goes on. "I know that I have caused you years of trouble, even though I never meant you harm. I know that right now, you're confused and don't know entirely who to trust. I beg you—ask your mother. About what happened, and about me. She was there." There's a pause, and I can tell he's unsure whether he should go on. But he does. "And she and I have met."

I feel a surge of bitter anger. "My mother abandoned me."

"No. She was driven away, to protect her own life." He

pauses. "Marina, leave that place. You are in danger there. Come to my hotel, and we will leave town together."

"Why do you want the child?" I demand, because that, above everything else, shocks me. I understand his guilt over what he did to me. If he was remorseless I wouldn't even bother speaking to him.

"I was told I could never be a father. I have wanted for years to retire from this life and try to have something more normal. A wife. Children. A quiet home." His voice is growing more impassioned. "And it is one more reason why I must protect you."

I swallow hard and glance at the door. Now and again I have to check to make sure there's no shadow moving back and forth under it. My uncle likes to eavesdrop.

"Even if I wanted to leave, I can't. I'm too fragile. I have to stay home and get better."

"Marina. Your therapist was hired by your father and is paid by your uncle. He is serving an agenda. They are not delusions just because he tells you that they are."

He adds, with a little laugh, "And you are far from fragile. Getting through this must have taken you more strength than I can imagine."

I look over at the diary and open it to the scrawled entry. "My father didn't hire Dr. Weiss, though. He was already dead when I was referred."

"That's not what Dr. Weiss' notes say."

My hand goes dead still above the page. "What did you say?"

He tells me.

I have a huge head of steam by the time I walk into Dr. Weiss's office the next morning. The temperature's risen above freezing; the melting ice from the eaves drips on me as I go through the front door of the three-story building. I don't even notice.

I'm having the same damn nightmares that I've had for five

years; I have a witness saying that my mother can verify that my "delusions" are anything but; and I just found out that I'm pregnant. I am in absolutely no mood to swallow anyone's bullshit.

"I want a copy of my file," I say firmly as I sit down, with no preamble.

Dr. Weiss is a soft-eyed man with an enormous mustache, white hair he seems to comb with an eggbeater, and a dull expression that crumbles into worry at my statement. "Those contain copies of my session notes. They're for my use, and it won't help your recovery to view them."

"You know, I just came from a doctor's office, and I had a talk with their HIPPA specialist while I was waiting for test results." I look him right in the eye. He's not used to this, and it clearly makes him nervous. I plow on. "If you kept your notes separate from my case file, you could use any explanation you want to keep them from me using that argument. But you didn't, so you can't."

He gapes at me. I have never lectured him before. I've always just accepted whatever he's told me, believing that he had my best interests at heart.

It makes me furious … and that fury makes me feel incredibly strong. "Bottom line: if I have to come back with a lawyer, it will be an opening salvo in a fat malpractice lawsuit."

"Marina," he laughs nervously, "where is all this coming from? Maybe you should calm down."

I close my eyes, struggling to focus through my anger. How many years have I depended on him to tell me what is real and what isn't? How many times have I let him hypnotize me?

Armand says that this man has been lying to me the whole time. Now, I need to test that theory.

"I'm sorry to have to take a hard line about this. But everything is changing, and I need to know that I can trust you." For a moment there's a note of pleading in my voice.

This doctor was my rock for a while. Now, seeing his wide fake smile and fearful eyes, I hate him with my whole heart.

"Just let me see my file. Print a copy out for me. I'll pay any fees you want, and we'll just go on from there."

His Adam's apple bobs above his collar. "No."

The hatred detonates inside me. "Then answer me this: how much money did my father pay you to convince me that my memories of his crimes are a damn delusion?"

He goes white as a ghost. "I-I-I don't know what you're talking about."

I close my eyes again and tears leak through my lashes. "Yes, you do. You're the opposite of a healer, you disgusting quack." I get up abruptly and grab my purse and coat. "And I'm sick of listening to your lies."

I call Armand while I'm walking to my car. "I'm going home to pack. Where should I meet you?"

"Crown Plaza, downtown, suite 418. What happened?"

"Dr. Weiss won't share my file. I called him on his shit and he fell apart. He's in on it. You're right about everything."

"Wait! Don't go—" he starts, but I hang up, because I've started choking on my tears.

"This is crazy, child," Anne says later, as she helps me pack. "Now I've got to pack you up and sneak you out before your uncle comes home. Is this guy really worth it?"

"It's a lot of things, not just him or the baby. I need to get away from my uncle for a while, Anne, and clear my head. I can't heal my problems while I'm dealing with his."

"I understand. And you know I'll always help you. Just like I promised when your mama left."

I pause. I've never asked her about my mother. Dr. Weiss always urged to me to move on from the abandonment and not even think about contacting her. "Anne, do you know why she left?"

She smiles a little. "You must be getting better if you're asking that. It's a long story. Let me go get your other suitcase from the coat room and I'll be right back."

She opens the door to walk out—and I see a familiar meaty hand yank her through the doorway as she lets out a startled yelp. "Ouch!" she cries. "Dr. Shea, what is that needle?"

She stumbles into the room and falls against the wall, sliding down onto her butt with a thud. Her eyes are glazed. "You drugged me," she manages, before going limp.

Uncle Bradley comes through the door and tosses an empty syringe at Anne's feet as she goes unconscious. I stare at him in growing horror as he draws out a full one and advances on me.

"Dr. Weiss gave me a call. Apparently you're too stupid to find your own assassin. I knew our little charade with the hypnosis would never work long-term, but it seems I'll have to deal with you myself, now." He licks his lips, a psychotic gleam in his eye. "So, on to plan B. I'm sure your organs will sell well."

I back away from him, horrified. *Of course my father's partner in crime would be his brother.* All this time he's been keeping me close. Paying a hypnotist to alter my memories. *Watching me.*

And grooming me to destroy myself by going after the very assassin he hired to do me in.

"It was you all along," I breathe as the pieces snap together in my head painfully, like bones being set.

"Yep," he replies cheerily. "Time to go to the basement, Marina."

CHAPTER FIFTEEN

Armand

It takes every ounce of willpower I have to keep to the speed limit as I drive to Marina's rescue. All I can think about is what her uncle will do to her once it reaches his ears that his psychological con-job hasn't stuck. *She's a witness. He'll kill her himself before she can go to the police.*

That can't happen.

By the time I reach their fancy stone villa, the sun has almost set. I know Marina must be home by now. Alone. Vulnerable. *Carrying my child in her belly.*

I wish I could have just told her up front about her uncle and what I suspected about her psychiatrist. But they set traps in her head to turn her away from the truth—even if it was right in front of her. I'm only lucky that she never mentioned meeting me.

The door is locked and alarmed. There's a conspicuous lack of staff around. I clamber up a rose trellis and slip in through a second floor window.

Almost at once, I hear the sounds of a fight coming from down the hall. Pulling one of Marina's Walthers from beneath my coat, I go racing toward it. I'm about to burst through the open door where the sounds are coming from when a tall, fat figure staggers out of it and falls against the wall.

It's Bradley. His face is swelling on one side and his eyes are wide with horror.

My fear for Marina turns into mirth as she stomps out after him and kicks him hard in the stomach. A syringe flies from his hand and shatters on the floor. "You sick, murdering, lying, fucking bastard!"

I can't help it. I burst into mocking laughter.

Both of them look over at me, startled. And then Marina—untouched, angry little Marina, who has trained for years to kill a professional assassin and is beyond fearing some soft, lazy old man—smiles at me. "You made it."

"Wouldn't miss it. What happened?"

"She attacked me!" blubbers Bradley, though no one asked him.

"You stupid bastard. It was your idea to have me go after Armand! Don't you think I'd learn to fight if I knew I was facing a seasoned assassin?" She's yelling at him like he's the stupidest lump of cowardly human meat on the planet, which seems pretty accurate right now.

I'm so fucking proud. She's not broken or helpless. She just had people lying to her for so long and so expertly that she believed it. But now, she's back.

"Well, yes," he blubbers. "But I never expected you to get good at it!"

"Happy to surprise you then, you prick." She turns to me. "I'll need to call the police and an ambulance for Anne. You should probably make yourself scarce soon. I'll meet you later."

"No!" Bradley explodes, and yanks a small revolver from his robe pocket. "I am not going to jail!"

I level the Walther at him. "Drop it."

He freezes and looks at me with the gun half raised, his red face coated in sweat and crocodile tears, and then looks over at Marina. His voice goes pleading as his expression crumples. "They were just homeless people! Better people needed their organs! We were saving lives!"

"You were making a profit, you pile of shit," Marina spits at him.

He screams in anguish—and moves fast. I'm faster, but when I see who he's aiming at I let him pull the damn trigger.

Sometimes you have to let the trash take itself out.

As his body slumps to the floor, dead of his own cowardice, I step past him and gather Marina into my arms. She hugs me back tightly. "Are you all right?" I whisper in her ear.

"I think I pulled a muscle or two kicking his ass," she says casually, but I can sense the exhaustion and fear behind her sarcasm. My arms tighten around her and she tucks her head under my chin. "I'll be okay. But Anne needs our help. She's been drugged."

I glance down at the woman lying just inside the bedroom door. She's breathing steadily and her eyelids flutter. "Looks like a tranquilizer. It's best if you make that call."

She looks up at me. "I don't want you to go."

"Meet me at the hotel when it's done. You can do this. But you won't be able to do it if half of Denver PD is chasing me around."

She nods and sighs. "I understand. I'll see you there."

It's hard to walk away, even with the danger over. I don't want her facing the police, the hospital, the press, any of it alone. But she's already proven that she doesn't need me.

She just wants me. Unexpectedly. Maybe undeservedly. And even with all the madness that just happened, that's the best feeling in the world.

SIGN UP TO RECEIVE A FREE BOOK

Sign Up to Receive Free E-Books and Audiobook Codes.

Would you like to read **The Unexpected Nanny, Dirty Little Virgin** and **other romance books** for **free**?

You can sign up to receive these free e-books and audiobooks by typing this link into your browser:

https://www.steamyromance.info/free-books-and-audiobooks-hot-and-steamy/

Or this one:

https://www.steamyromance.info/the-unexpected-nanny-free/

PREVIEW OF SAVING HER RESCUER

A Billionaire & A Virgin Romance

By Michelle Love

∽

Blurb

Bethany

I was just trying to get away from my crazy ex for the weekend when I ended up in a giant pileup on the highway up to Gore Mountain. I wasn't hurt, but I was trapped in my car. Then this guy shows up out of nowhere, frees me, carries me to safety … then calls me by the wrong name and disappears before I can thank him. I've got to find out who this hot, mysterious older guy is. Who is Henry Frakes, and why did he call me Cara? And when things heat up between us, is it me he's seeing in his arms ... or her?

Blurb

Henry

She's the very image of the wife I lost twenty years ago on that same damned stretch of road. But Bethany's her own person, and I'm still dealing with the scars of that terrible day. When I got stuck in that pileup, I ended up in a flashback. But this time, I saved Cara. Until I came out of it and realized that I had rescued someone else. Maybe I have a type. Maybe Bethany is Cara reincarnated. I have demons to battle before I can claim Bethany as my own, but they're all inside my head ... mostly.

CHAPTER ONE

Bethany

I make my way up to Gore Mountain as soon as the roads are clear, thinking only of getting out of Boston. It's a chilly five-hour drive to the Adirondacks, but I don't care. That's five hours between me and my battered apartment with its boarded-over window and punch marks in one wall—and between me and Michael, who did the damage.

I knew we wouldn't last when he started flirting with my classmates, but I never expected him to melt down completely like this when I dumped him. *And after I caught him cheating in our own bed!*

The fading bruise under my eye still stings after three days. Michael committed two deal-breakers in the span of two hours that night. One of them got him a night in jail, and an emergency protection order against him.

He knows we're quits. But he refuses to let go. This morning I caught him waiting outside my door in the apartment hallway He even had the balls to be pissed that I changed the locks.

So, he's spending another few nights in jail, for violating the protection order. And I'm taking a badly-needed break from Boston.

I couldn't sleep comfortably in my apartment with so many reminders of Michael around. So I pulled out a chunk of my savings, made a hotel reservation, and took off for the Adirondacks.

I reach the highway and the traffic thins, and I breathe a sigh of relief. I hate driving in Boston. The motorists there practically *try* to hit each other.

But that's where school is, and home until I'm done with school. I was lucky to get my apartment—just like I'm lucky that my internship, scholarship money and the money from my blog add up to enough to pay for it. So I manage, for now.

My idea of a break always involves getting out of town for a while, and away from the press of people. This time, the feeling is just a bit more urgent than usual. *Thanks, Michael, you horse's ass.*

I've missed Gore Mountain for years. I haven't had the cash to visit much since I left home, but I have always dreamed of coming back. I used to ski myself sore there every winter: sore and sunburnt and numb-nosed from the icy wind whipping by.

There's no more peaceful feeling for me than racing down a mountain slope alone.

I'm hoping to recapture it this weekend, and cleanse my aching heart. That's the reason I'm risking going up there so soon after a round of unseasonably heavy snowstorms. At least the temperature's already rising above freezing.

I feel my spirits lift as I put some music on and prepare myself mentally for the long haul ahead. *Between the fresh snow on the slopes, the warmer spring weather and the thinner crowds, the resort should be lovely for unwinding.*

That damned idiot Michael will still be trying to call me once they let him out, but I can screen my calls. He constantly violates the protection order, no matter how often he gets reported and picked up for it. Yet another reason for me to get out of town for a while.

Go to Hell, Michael. If he keeps this garbage up, he can see how well his uselessness, whining and abusive bullshit goes over in General Population.

I start to really relax after about the first hour of driving. I stop poking at my bruise, some of the tension leaves my muscles, and I even catch myself humming along to AC/DC on the radio. By the time I stop for lunch at a tiny roadside diner three hours into my drive, I'm even smiling.

See? I tell myself as I pull into the parking lot. *You can do this. Life can go on. It didn't end when Michael lost his shit and started breaking things.*

The diner is a weird steak and burger place with rustic timber decor and a mobster theme. Movie posters line the walls: *The Godfather, King of New York, Prizzi's Honor*. A badly edited TV version of *Goodfellas* plays on the television.

A line-faced waitress with red-dyed hair and too much makeup smiles at me as she brings me a menu and some water. I sip it as I page through the offerings.

I almost order the diet plate on reflex: salad and an unappetizing-sounding ground turkey patty. But then I remember *Michael's gone* and smile, and order a bacon cheeseburger.

How many times did we eat out only for him to stare at me and make disapproving noises when I ate more than would sustain a kitten? Every damn time. He wanted me bony, but I don't skinny down that much without getting sick.

So now, I'm going to enjoy myself a little. Maybe I'll even have a milkshake. I'll be burning it off on the slopes soon enough.

Now that I have left Boston behind, it's like a weight has

lifted off of me. I got a little too used to the burden of Michael, I realize. Now that I'm free, I feel myself coming to life inside.

And suddenly I'm horny as hell.

Sex with Michael was about as satisfying as gas station pizza: unexciting, barely filling, without real nourishment, and sometimes a little bit sickening. As I look around the half-filled cafe at the truckers and tourists who have also stopped for a bite, my eyes trace over every unaccompanied man with the excited curiosity of the newly free.

Well. All except the young blond guy. Michael has killed my taste for that type, probably for good.

That's fine; the lodge will be full of athletic men, and some will be single. *I'm free of him. I can look around. Date. Get laid by someone who actually knows and cares about what he's doing.*

What an intriguing idea. Also a first for me, but I know men like that are actually out there. I've heard my girl friends raving about this or that wild weekend, and one or two are already planning their weddings. I've just had crappy luck, I guess.

That's okay. *My time will come. Maybe even this weekend.*

What I really want is a rare animal: a guy who actually treats me well *and* has skill and patience in bed. That probably means someone older than me, way more mature than boys my age, and more...experienced.

But will I be able to attract someone like that? The only problem with older guys is that so many of them seem to be looking for someone naive as well as young and hot. I haven't been naive in years; just too kind-hearted for my own good.

I follow my burger up with a mocha as I watch the room, then get back on the road once my meal settles. I'm headed up into the Adirondacks now, and the snow I left behind in Boston now starts to streak the sides of the road again as I gain elevation.

Soon enough, I reach the real snow country, up where the

plows are still working, and the wind blows clouds of shimmering white off the slopes above. The new snowfall has loaded down the evergreens that flank the road so thickly that their branches bend toward the ground. Sometimes, the quickly-melting burden slides off in chunks, and the dark green branches bound skyward, throwing the rest off in glittering arcs.

Now and again, my car passes a clear slope that gleams like a pearl in the strengthening sun. I can't wait to get my skis on when I see them. But we're still a ways from Gore Mountain yet, and I need to be patient, and focus on the road.

The traffic starts thickening as I get closer to the resort. I slow down, ignoring the honks from impatient people behind me. The snow has redeposited on the highway in places, making it slippery and treacherous.

Now and again, a fresh cloud of snow overtakes the road briefly, blown by the wind that screams down the slopes and sometimes makes my car rock. I cut on my fog lights and slow down further, wary of a spring avalanche. You don't fall in love with the snow without understanding all the ways that it can kill you.

The guy right behind me keeps laying on his horn, not seeming to notice how the blown snow from off the mountain keeps getting thicker around us. I pull to the side and let his battered SUV roar past, and he yells something obnoxious at me in a Jersey accent. *Yeah, yeah, asshole. Try not to drive off the cliff.*

Then something strange happens. The cloud of white in front of me suddenly becomes so dense that it seems to swallow the SUV entirely, along with every car near it. I frown, slowing further—and suddenly hear the scream of tires and feel the ground start to shake.

Oh fuck! I brake and pull over—but too late. The rumble becomes a roar—and suddenly the screech of tires turns into shattering glass and tearing metal.

I try to back up but there's nowhere to go. The cars behind me are starting to smash into each other. I feel someone run into my back bumper, pushing me forward into the snow cloud.

"No!" I yank the wheel futilely. Chunks of wet snow slam against my windshield; I let out a scream of shock and fear. Then something hits the side of my car so hard that it goes tumbling side-over-side into the air...and right off the cliff's edge.

I hear a hard thud, and the crunch of glass. The seatbelt digs into my shoulder, and I black out.

CHAPTER TWO

Bethany

I open my eyes to an upside-down world. My windows are completely white outside but are amazingly intact; the car's functional enough that I can see the glow of the headlights faintly through the layer of snow. I'm conscious, alive..and in a crazy situation.

I flip on the emergency lights, praying someone will see them in the blowing snow, then do a quick check-in with myself. My head hurts, one shoulder feels wrenched, and I'm sure I'll have bruises from the seatbelt I'm hanging from. But I'm not bleeding, I can feel my feet, and nothing seems broken.

Holy shit. I close my eyes, trying to focus past my fear. *That was an avalanche. I just got hit by a damn avalanche and survived!*

So far, anyway.

"Okay," I tell myself, my voice strangely loud in the small space. "Emergency lights are on and flashing. This is a major highway. Rescue crews are coming.

"Someone will notice me. I'll be able to get air, and I'll be able to stay warm until they dig me out." I have to stop and draw a sobbing breath as I weather another wave of fear. "I'm only partly buried, and it's still daylight."

It's okay. I'll be free soon. Someone will come.

The onslaught of logic-based reassurances works well enough that I stop shaking. I finally take another deep breath and open my eyes. My head is pounding from being upside down, but I don't seem to have hit it.

Another plus: I don't smell gasoline.

I still have to get out of here. The sudden understanding hits me hard, along with the realization that drives it: what if there's another avalanche before someone can reach me? I could be knocked off whatever my car's come to rest on and go tumbling into the ravine. Or I could simply end up buried beyond recovery.

Yeah, fuck staying. I brace myself against the roof and unlatch my seatbelt, huffing slightly as I fall from it and bang my knees against the steering wheel. The avalanche hit me broadside; the trees on the slope of the ravine must have broken my car's fall. Fortunately, wherever my car is wedged, it is at least temporarily stable.

I reposition myself awkwardly in the small space, setting my shoulder against the door and shoving as I work its latch. It moves barely an inch—but then stops, wedged shut by the weight of the frozen mess beyond. "Fuck!"

I turn around and put my feet against the door, bracing myself and shoving against it with all the strength in my legs. It barely moves another inch; snow falls onto my ankles, and a little fresh air trickles in, but that's it. I'm completely trapped.

Tears of pure terror blur my vision for a moment. I dash them away and set my jaw, repeating my reassurances. *No need to panic. Someone will get to me. I just have to get their attention.*

Fortunately, the horn is still working.

I honk it in intervals: ten seconds on, ten seconds off to

nervously listen. During those desperate in-between times, I can hear distant, muffled noises: sirens, walkie-talkies, occasional cries of dismay. *How many people were hit by the avalanche, or piled up their cars because they couldn't stop in time?*

How many people died?

That thought makes me sick. Tears of fear and despair fill my eyes again, but I keep working the horn. *Whatever happens, I'm not going to join them!*

The battery will run out eventually. I'm terrified of what could happen then—when the horn goes silent and the lights go dark. The heater will stop working then too.

But I don't dare run the engine to recharge the battery. With no idea what shape it's in, I could start a fire.

This is not how I plan to go out, damn it! My breath shivers; I'm trembling. But I still fight to keep focused. *I can still survive. Someone will save me.*

Someone...please save me.

The horn is starting to lose its strength and the lights flicker and dim when I suddenly hear the crunch of footsteps coming toward me. Just one pair, heavy and purposeful. "Hello?" I call out at the top of my lungs, and then honk the horn again.

The footsteps walk right up to the driver's side of the car, and after a moment, I hear the snow crunch in a different way, and shift. Then again. Someone is digging.

I hold my breath, not wanting to distract the stranger with any more yelling and honking. The steady crunch of the shovel biting away chunks of snow grows closer, and eventually I can hear the low, masculine grunts of effort behind it.

Oh thank God, it must be a rescue worker. I sag with relief; they have finally gotten to me. Or...someone else has.

The shovel clacks hard against my driver's side window, and I flinch away from it. Whoever is digging me out pauses, and I see a black-gloved hand brush the last layer of snow away from the window.

A face peers in at me: long and handsome, with piercing green eyes that have crows' feet at the corners. He stares in at me with a stunned expression for a few seconds...and then straightens and starts digging the rest of the snow away from the door. His movements are frantic now, and I wait breathlessly for him to finish.

Finally, he tosses aside the shovel and grabs a crowbar out of the snowbank. I watch him use it to scrape the snow and ice away from the crack in the door, then laboriously pry it open.

Finally it opens with a jerk and I bolt forward, practically crashing into his legs in my effort to get out of that car. He drops the crowbar and catches me, wrapping his arms around me to steady me.

"It's all right, Cara," he mumbles in a deep, strangely distracted voice. "I've got you. I saved you this time."

"Oh God, that was crazy. Thank you." Then what he said registers and I blink up at him, completely lost. "Sorry, what?"

He smiles dreamily, then easily scoops me up. He's a big man, fit, his body broad-shouldered and hard under his insulated clothes. "We'll have the paramedics check you out, and then we'll go home. You'll be okay."

I don't protest; I feel wobbly suddenly, my muscles shaking. I'm still lost on why he called me Cara...but as he carries me up the steep, snow-clogged slope and onto the road, I'm suddenly too distracted to care.

The avalanche completely blocks the highway. Cars, trucks and SUVs are caught in it, twisted and sometimes smoking. The one that passed me up earlier is halfway down the ravine, fetched up against a shattered stand of trees.

I stare at the twisted shape, crushed like a beer can in a

drunk's fist, and my eyes blur with tears. *Why the hell didn't you slow down?*

Even worse is the pile-up just before the avalanche. At least ten cars lie all over the icy road, sometimes in pieces. Six ambulances, a search and rescue team and a highway team with digging equipment are all hard at work dealing with the mess.

I gasp in horror, and the stranger's grip tightens on me. "Shh, sh. It's okay, try to stay calm. We just have to make sure you're not hurt."

I nod mutely, burying my face against his strong shoulder. Three tow trucks pull away as he climbs over the mound of snow and crushed cars with me in his arms. I stare at the chewed-up messes the trucks are dragging and realize that I was incredibly lucky. Their occupants are probably dead.

I could be too, right now. But instead, I have my hero out of nowhere, with his gentle hands and hazy eyes. He keeps doggedly carrying me toward the small army of ambulances at the far end of the mess.

He smells really nice: woodsmoke, leather, bay rum aftershave. His breath smells like mint gum and coffee, and he cradles me against him like I'm something precious.

"What's your name?" I ask him, intrigued.

"You know my name, sweetheart," he murmurs with that distracted smile. I suddenly realize that he's in some kind of shock as well.

Oh shit. What's going on with this guy? "Are you okay?"

"I am now that I know you're safe. But I can't say the same for the Lexus." His voice is low and thoughtful, very serious—but his eyes stay hazed over, and I start to wonder if he's hit his head. At least his pupils are the same size.

"Maybe you should have the paramedics look at you too," I suggest very tentatively.

My hair blows into my eyes and he brushes it out of them

almost tenderly. I'm confused, liking the sensation but too overwhelmed to think about it much.

He plods on tirelessly. "I'll be fine. I don't have a scratch on me. Let's just get you checked out."

I keep quiet until he carries me easily over to an unoccupied ambulance. "Hey," he calls out. "I just peeled my lady here out of that upside-down Dodge. She was the one on the horn. Anyone free?"

He seems completely lucid now, and I'm...not, I realize. My legs and arms are shaking, and though my heart has slowed down, my whole body feels weak from all the adrenaline that has run through me.

The exhausted-looking crew members look up: two men and a woman, each nursing a coffee. One of the men downs his and sets his thermos aside to come help my rescuer bundle me into the back of the ambulance.

"How long were you trapped?" the shaven-headed guy asks as he takes my blood pressure.

"I don't know. It can't have been too long, my car still had power for a while." I squint as he shines a pen light in my eyes. "I was unconscious for a bit, but I think that was the shock."

"Any pain? Did you hit your head?"

"Not that I can remember." I answer his list of questions on autopilot as I look over at the man who saved me. He's watching me carefully, but has moved back, letting the medics do their work.

Who is he? He seems reluctant to give his name...but he also looks strangely familiar. Not very many guys are that memorable-looking. But where have I seen him before?

Miraculously, I still have my phone. I forgot it in all the chaos. I pull it out and snap a few photos of the guy.

Seeing me do that, he playfully pulls out his phone and does the same to me. The way he smiles...his tender manner. *Has he mistaken me for someone else?*

That has to be it. It's the only thing besides my totally misreading the situation that makes any sense. He's just a big, brave, charming flirt who's trying to keep me from falling into a panic or depression after rescuing me.

He could also be delusional in some way. But the way that his heroics, his kindness, his scent and his touch have all caught my attention make me *really* hope it's not that.

"Okay, you've suffered a bad shock, and some bruising, especially across your shoulder. The good news is, it's nothing ibuprofen, fluids and sleep won't fix. We're waiting for a transport bus to take everyone to town. Were you headed for the ski resort?" The paramedic hands me a cup of cocoa.

"Yeah," I murmur, still keeping an eye on the man who saved me. He's lowering his phone, and looks confused. "I have a reservation at the Gore Mountain Lodge."

When I look up again, Mystery Guy's on the phone talking to someone.

"You'll have to rent a car in town and move your stuff there tomorrow. For tonight we're putting everyone up at a local motel while the injured go to the hospital. Was there anyone with you besides your husband?"

I look up at the paramedic suddenly, feeling my cheeks burn. "Oh, uh, he's not my husband. He just saved me. Came out of nowhere, actually."

"Huh." He frowns over at the man, who seems to be arguing with someone. Then he grabs a clipboard and hands it to me. "Okay, well, here you go.

"Just put down your contact information and the details about your car. We're gonna haul it off for you. We'll drop it at the mechanic's if it can't be driven. Otherwise we'll bring it to the motel parking lot."

"Thank you," I manage, feeling a slow trickle of relief. This is crazy, and scary, and disruptive, but it is only a setback. I will be all right. I can drive up to the resort and go skiing tomorrow, if I'm not too sore.

I look up to thank my rescuer as well—and blink in shock, looking around. He's gone...just as suddenly as he arrived.

CHAPTER THREE

Henry

"It was Cara. I swear to God that it was, Uncle Jake."

Jake's been making us dinner while he listens to the news on his phone. The avalanche and the crash are all over it right now. He looks up from rough-chopping a length of pepperoni, his expression pained.

"Henry...Cara's dead. You know that."

I take a deep breath. He said the same thing to me on the phone, while I was looking right at her. Cara, my love, my wife, whom I buried almost twenty years ago.

I saved you this time, I think, licking my dry, chilled lips as a sense of unreality washes over me. *I finally managed it.*

Logically, I know that my uncle's right. His hard, worried look drags my feet back onto the ground: flight of fancy over.

Not my wife at all. Too young, and way too...alive. But how the Hell do you explain this?

"I know," I say, holding my hands up. "You're right. Cara's been dead for two decades now, and I know that.

"But this woman literally looked just like her. Same hair, same eyes, same build—"

"You had a flashback, Henry," he says with just the slightest edge of frustration to his voice. "You rescued some woman because you thought she was Cara. But she wasn't. Now please, tell me you really know that."

I sigh in exasperation, and pull out my phone. I unlock it, pull up the photos I took of her, and hand it over to him. "Here. See for yourself."

He sets down his knife, then slowly takes the phone. His eyes widen as he stares down at the first photo. "Holy shit."

He looks up at me, blinking slowly, then looks back down at the phone screen again. "...Okay. I get it, I'm lots less worried about your mental state now—but that is genuinely fucking weird."

"The woman I rescued *does* look exactly like my Cara." *I'm not crazy—or at least, not quite that crazy.*

"So much so that I'm wondering if Cara had a cousin. But this girl's too young. Did you get her name?" He's still staring at me piercingly, as if still not quite trusting my grip on reality.

I can't blame him, even if I resent his doubts sometimes. Losing Cara broke me, and he's the one who has been helping me put the pieces back together. But today, my progress got seriously challenged.

That crash threw me into the most profound flashback I have had in six years. Suddenly, I was back in my truck with Cara, everything shattered around us: Cara unconscious and bleeding from the head. But a moment later, I was alone in my smashed Lexus surrounded by deployed airbags, and she was gone.

So I went looking for her. And I found that girl instead. "Yeah, I was flashing back, but can you blame me? She was real, and she really looked like...that."

Like my Cara. Lovely Cara, my wife of eighteen months, whom I married just out of high school. It makes me ache just thinking about it.

We were both dizzily in love, and had no idea that forces had already been set in motion to rip her from my arms for good. No idea that it would be my own mistakes that would force me to stumble on without her, heart and mind in pieces. But that is exactly what happened, and ever since then, I've lived with the guilt.

Today, though, I almost feel like I started working off my crime. It doesn't bring Cara back, but an innocent girl with her face is now alive thanks to me.

I've really got Uncle Jake's attention now. He seems a lot less worried...but a lot more confused. "That's one hell of a mindfuck. Did you get her name?"

I shake my head, regretting it. "No. I was too disoriented...especially once you and I started arguing over the phone. Not that I'm blaming you. I wish I had gotten her name and phone number."

He lets out a low grunt, looking thoughtful, then peers at me. "What happened to the Lexus? You hurt?" He hands me back my phone and goes back to chopping.

"Totaled. But the safety measures did their job. I could use a trip to my chiropractor, but that's it."

"That was lucky. What shape is the girl's car in?" He finishes with the pepperoni and starts chopping mushrooms and a few kinds of olives together.

I sit down at the kitchen table, mouth watering. I know better than to get in his way when he's cooking. He's territorial in the kitchen. "Upside down in a snowbank ten feet down the slope. Good thing she was wearing her seatbelt at the time."

Unlike Cara. God, Cara... I shake it off, and look down at the tired, bruised girl on my phone. Not Cara, but real, and her spitting image. And safe now, because of me.

Shocked, flashing back, and I still managed to save someone's life. That's not bad at all.

My uncle chops away, keeping half an eye on me. "Sounds like the poor kid had a really shitty day. But it probably would have been worse if you weren't there."

"I was just thinking that." *Bruised.* I peer distractedly at the image. "That's strange."

"Eh? What's that?" He pauses in his work again and looks my way.

"The bruise under her eye is developed. Maybe a few days old." The sleuth in me, lover of true crime novels and whodunit movies, focuses in on the detail. "...That's a shiner."

Someone hit her.

The sudden, intense surge of rage takes me completely by surprise. I know in the back of my head that it's because she looks like Cara. The idea of someone slamming his fist into that face makes me want to find him, and beat him until he can't move.

"Henry." My uncle's voice is sharp.

"It looks like she was attacked." *I should do something. If not to him, then for her.*

"Leave it, Henry."

I look up at him, a mix of puzzled and annoyed. "What?"

He sighs through his nose. "Leave it. She is a complete stranger, and it is her business. Let me make the goddamn calzones, let's have supper, and let's watch *The Maltese Falcon* like normal people.

"I know she looks like Cara. I know you miss that girl so much that you haven't touched another woman since. I know you punish yourself all the damn time, too."

He took a deep breath, and stared at me pointedly. "If having helped this girl makes you hate yourself a little less, then good for you. But don't go chasing her."

That shouldn't piss me off, but it does. She can't have been put in my path for no reason. It's too much of a coincidence that a girl the very image of my dead wife should end up in a car accident on the same stretch of road, only to be rescued by me.

Do I believe in reincarnation? I have never even considered it before today. But even if that crazy theory is somehow right, do I have any right to chase after some new incarnation of Cara, after failing her so badly last time?

Whoever this girl is, if I come at her with all of this, she would probably think I'm completely crazy. I might even scare her away completely. And what would it accomplish?

I may not even have the right to pursue her. My task may simply have been to save her this time, and be satisfied that she is alive and happy in the world somewhere.

But then the image of the bruise on her cheek rises in my mind, and my fists clench on the tabletop. *Is she happy, though? Is she safe?*

"You're not saying anything," my uncle observes as he finishes chopping olives.

"I'm just wondering if she's doing okay."

The knife thwacks against the chopping block a little too hard. "Henry. For the last time, this is not good for you. You want to end up with a restraining order against you for scaring some stranger because you miss your wife? This self-punishing shit has to stop."

He's right. I know it in my gut. I will probably alarm the girl if I go tracking her down.

Fuck. My heart sinks as I think about it, but I finally sigh and nod. "You're right. I won't pursue her. But I sure am curious why she looks so much like Cara."

I see his shoulders sag with relief, and he goes right back to kitchen prep. "Good. So am I, but you know how you get."

"Yeah." *But what about the bruise?* "I know how I get."

That evening, having missed my afternoon workout, I make up for it brutally, filling my home gym with a hard-rock soundtrack and the clangs, thumps and pulley-creaks of exercise equipment. I've been obsessed with fitness since junior high, when I learned how a well-toned body and some practice could protect both myself and Cara from the neighborhood bullies.

We met and made friends in seventh grade after I moved in with my uncle. Back then, our family was poor, and his veteran's pension allowed him a small house in Poughkeepsie, and nothing more. She lived just down the road, and walked past my house every morning on her way to school.

I realized that she was being bullied when she asked me to walk with her. I was shy, but one look at the fear in those velvety eyes and I had to help her. Two years later she gave me my first kiss, and after that, I belonged to her.

I learned to fight, and worked out daily, with an extra run at night. I ate so much boiled chicken, eggs and yogurt those days that I started getting stomach aches. I wanted to make myself huge, a bulwark between Cara and the world.

Today, I run ten miles a day, or bike twenty. I have an hour of weight training, and an hour of judo practice. My routine back then was even more brutal.

I chuckle a little as I do crunches on my slant board, remembering. My abdominals gleam with sweat as they bunch and flex. These days, I'm pretty satisfied with my looks, speed and strength.

Back then, I was constantly frustrated, because I was building on a base of junior high reediness. Being an impressionable teen, I was also basing my expectations on the bodies I saw in comics and film—with teen boys drawn as or played by twenty-something men. So I was never satisfied with what I saw in the mirror.

But Cara was. The night she surprised me with that kiss, my heart walked off after her like a puppy. We were fifteen.

I started working out harder, joining the weight training class, track, martial arts courses. I wanted to look good for her. I wanted her to want to touch me.

We were sixteen when her scumbag father caught me walking her back from school. He demanded to know what I was doing and I explained about the big guys who kept lifting up her skirt at the bus stop. He somehow convinced himself I was gay because I didn't participate, and only because of that, trusted me with his daughter.

A year later, Cara slipped in my bedroom window after climbing up the rose trellis. For the first time, we could touch each other as much as we wanted. Giddy with excitement, trying to keep our voices down, we struggled to strip each other down under the covers. And then...

I groan through my teeth as I work through the last of my set. My memories have left my cock hard and throbbing, tenting my indigo workout shorts. I miss her even more now, and wonder again about the girl with her face.

Thoughts of her haunt me through my workout. I wonder if she would enjoy the same things in bed that Cara did. *That's a dangerous train of thought,* I warn myself, and try to focus on my workout.

A sauna and a cool shower leave me relaxed and sleepy enough for a novel and bed. I'm working my way through *Never Cry Wolf*. It's a much better read than expected, even compared to the movie, which is one of my favorites.

But as I struggle to enjoy it, my mind keeps going back to Cara's twin, with the haunted eyes and bruised face. My thoughts linger on her until I fall asleep.

We've been kissing for hours, our hearts beating wildly against each other as I revel in the feel of her soft, naked breasts against my chest. How did she know Uncle Jake would leave for his flight at ten, and would be gone for the whole weekend?

She came here. She took the risk. She came to me, and she brought condoms.

I can't believe my luck as I run my hands over her warm, soft curves, helping her wiggle out of her clothes. Her eyes stare up at me in the moonlight, bright with desire and trust. "I want you to do it," she whispers as she unties the drawstring of my sleep shorts. "I want you to do everything."

I almost blast my first load right into the fabric at her invitation, but manage to control my eagerness. Still, I'm overwhelmed—with her, with my gorgeous, brave girlfriend, who snuck in like a thief to bring me the night of my dreams.

I tremble on top of her, one thigh wedged between her legs and my hand running over the gorgeous, springy globe of her breast. I run my thumb over the nipple and she gasps aloud.

"Mm, feels good..." she whimpers, and I start stroking that tiny, silky nub of flesh, watching it tighten as she throws her head back and pants.

It's amazing. I sit up on my knees over her and start fingering both of them. She squirms, arching her back, her eyes wide with amazement. "Oh!" she cries, and I muffle her with my mouth as she whimpers and squeals.

My erection's so hard now that it hurts. I feel it throbbing against my belly through the fabric. Now and again, her squirming body brushes up against it, and I grunt into her mouth as I feel a tingle shoot through my body.

I break the kiss and move downward as she keeps writhing, enjoying the sounds of her trying to muffle her own gasps and moans behind her lips. Her body bucks under mine, offering the glorious softness of her breasts as I hover over them hungrily. Finally, unable to stand it, I start kissing her nipple, running my hand down her body instead.

Her body stiffens; she presses her breast against my mouth and I pounce on it, suckling eagerly. The taste of her skin, her softness, her trilling croons as she grabs double handfuls of my hair and starts to buck her hips, they all intoxicate me.

I slide an arm under her, propping myself on my elbow as I suckle her breast and feel her tremble and thrash under me. Her voice has gone to wordless, musical cries; she finally drags over a pillow and buries her face in it. I suck harder and hear her muffled squeal.

My hand finally works between us, pulling her panties down and shoving my shorts down to free my cock. She lifts her hips to help me, her thighs parting as she kicks free of the thin cotton...and then settling around me.

Everything in me aches to thrust into her, but somehow, I remember the condom. Rolling it on seems to take a million years as she pants and moans under me. My mouth works over her nipple, and then shifts and fastens onto the other just as I finish rolling the rubber over my pounding shaft.

My free hand drifts to her soft, sparsely-haired pussy, now slick with her juices, and I part her gently with my fingers. She pumps her hips harder as I stroke her. I look up, and see her head stretched back, every muscle taut as I suckle and caress.

Her body trembles, so tense that she practically lifts me off the bed. Her warm pussy bucks invitingly against my hand. Finally, unable to stand it, I fit the sheathed head of my cock into her warm opening and thrust into her.

Her nails rake my shoulders; she lets out a long moan—and my hand and mouth move on autopilot as her body takes my cock into its warm, slick embrace. I groan hoarsely against her breast, and then start thrusting in time with my caresses.

It's so good. Her body embraces me again and again as I sink into her, my hips pumping slowly...then faster and faster. Her legs tighten around me; I can barely remember to keep fingering her, but I manage somehow.

Her flesh starts to clench around me as her cries reach their peak; she goes up on her heels—and then grinds and shudders around me violently as I lose control and pound into her hard. I hear her voice from far away, calling out with joy—and then I soar up to join her.

I wake covered in hot sweat and groan, feeling my cock pumping out its load so hard it almost hurts. "*Cara—*" I gasp before I can stop myself. My hips thrust upward hard—and then I collapse to the mattress, shaking and tingling.

Oh, Baby, oh sweetheart...I miss you so fucking much.

It's been twenty years since I touched a woman. My sex drive hasn't exactly gone dormant...but I haven't had a dream like that in years. As I drag myself up and shower off, I wonder again: *who is she, this woman with my wife's face?*

If you want to continue reading this story, you can get your copy from your favorite vendor by searching for the title:

Saving her Rescuer: A Billionaire & A Virgin Romance

You can also find the e-book version by typing this link in your computer's browser:

https://www.hotandsteamyromance.com/collections/ frontpage/products/saving-her-rescuer-a-billionaire-a-virgin- romance

ABOUT THE AUTHOR

Mrs. Love writes about smart, sexy women and the hot alpha billionaires who love them. She has found her own happily ever after with her dream husband and adorable 6 and 2 year old kids.

Currently, Michelle is hard at work on the next book in the series, and trying to stay off the Internet.

"Thank you for supporting an indie author. Anything you can do, whether it be writing a review, or even simply telling a fellow reader that you enjoyed this. Thanks

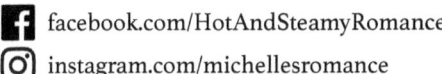 facebook.com/HotAndSteamyRomance
instagram.com/michellesromance

©Copyright 2020 by Michelle Love - All rights Reserved
In no way is it legal to reproduce, duplicate, or transmit any part of this document in either electronic means or in printed format. Recording of this publication is strictly prohibited and any storage of this document is not allowed unless with written permission from the publisher. All rights are reserved.
Respective authors own all copyrights not held by the publisher.

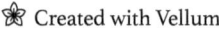 Created with Vellum

www.ingramcontent.com/pod-product-compliance
Lightning Source LLC
LaVergne TN
LVHW011725060526
838200LV00051B/3026